another life

Frank McGinty lives near Glasgow with his wife, daughter and two sons. He worked as a principal guidance teacher in a Glasgow comprehensive, but recently gave that up to give talks in schools and to concentrate on writing. He has written two non-fiction books for teenagers. This is his first novel.

He enjoys going to the theatre, meeting new people in schools, and going on holiday as often as possible! You can check out his website at www.frankmcginty.com.

Also available by Frank McGinty from Piccadilly Press:

Smart Thinking!
Take the Sting Out of Study

another life

frank mcginty

Piccadilly Press • London

*To all in Iona House at Notre Dame High School,
Glasgow. Thanks for the memories!*

First published in Great Britain in 2003
by Piccadilly Press Ltd.,
5 Castle Road, London NW1 8PR

A catalogue record for this book is available
from the British Library

ISBN: 1 85340 703 8 (trade paperback)

1 3 5 7 9 10 8 6 4 2

Printed and bound in Great Britain by Bookmarque Ltd
Typeset by Textype Typesetters
Cover design by Fielding Design
Set in Goudy

Prologue

Saturday morning. The blue sky and the sunlight that filtered through her bedroom window indicated to Jane that the heatwave was holding. She got out of bed, opened the window wide and breathed in the fresh morning air. Today she had a reason to feel good. Today was her sixteenth birthday.

She took a long, leisurely shower, and let her mind drift back to past birthdays. Family birthdays were different when her mother was alive. Just like Christmas, only on birthdays it was Christmas for one. Presents were wrapped and left overnight on the settee, so that she or her brother, Barry, would see them first thing in the morning. Later in the day there would be a special meal, with all kinds of treats and always a cake with just the right number of candles.

Jane sighed contentedly as she dried her hair. She laughed to herself when she remembered that on her birthdays she usually ended up feeling sick! During the day she'd tuck into the birthday chocolates, and at dinner there would be her favourite dessert, mint Vienetta. Afterwards she would go with the family and a few chosen friends to the cinema or the bowling alley or whatever. Then she had to oblige her parents by stuffing her face with a huge wedge of birthday cake. All for a good cause, of course.

As she slipped into her top and shorts, Jane's feeling of contentment suddenly turned to rage as the manner of her Mum's death came flooding back to her. She quickly turned her thoughts back to birthdays, but her anger didn't pass. Her dad and Barry had forgotten her last two birthdays. After all she had done for them. Not only was she taken for granted, she was completely forgotten too! But she had high hopes for this birthday. She'd dropped hints for weeks so that they could get their act together.

She pulled on her sandals and tiptoed quietly downstairs. She was always the first up, and she didn't like to disturb the others. When she opened the living room door, her heart sank.

There wasn't a present in sight, but it was more than that – it was the state of the place. The coffee table was covered with empty beer cans. Cigarette ends had spilled over the single ashtray and littered the carpet, like spent cartridges from a machine gun. A bottle of cheap fortified wine had toppled next to one of the chairs and the stale stench from the damp patch was nauseating. The forlorn remnants of a Chinese takeaway were scattered everywhere, making their own contribution to the foul atmosphere.

Dad brought home some of his cronies from the pub and they had a night of it, she thought. Again.

She knew that if she didn't clear up the mess it would lie there festering away. If only Mum could see this! she said to herself.

I'm glad I slept through this, Jane thought as she began clearing up. She had gone to bed early the night before, and as usual had slept soundly. The only time she had when she didn't think about anything was when she was sleeping.

It was after midday before her dad emerged from his room. He appeared in the kitchen wearing trousers and a vest, the black stubble on his chin contrasting sharply with the pallor of his skin.

'The Grim Reaper comes to call,' said Jane.

'Aw, don't be like that, darlin'. That's the last time that lot will ever get back here, I promise you.'

'Oh, sure! Of course it is,' said Jane in her best patronising tone.

'My God, is that the time?' he asked. 'You couldn't nip along to the bookie's with a line, could you? This one's a cert, and you'll get a share of the winnings.'

For a moment Jane thought the promise of cash might be some kind of acknowledgement of her birthday, but the blank look on her dad's face told her that wasn't the case. She couldn't believe it. Sixteen! A special birthday. Even under Scottish law she now had more rights than she had twenty-four hours ago – she could leave home, leave school, get married, open a full bank account and apply for loans if she wanted to – and her very own father had forgotten.

Before Jane could feel any more sorry for herself, Barry barged into the kitchen. If anything he looked even more haggard than his dad. 'Like father, like son,' muttered Jane.

'Any chance of a bite to eat?' he asked.

'Help yourself! And you can forget the bookie's,' snapped Jane, turning to face her father. Her pent up fury needed an outlet. 'I'm getting out of here for a while!'

She climbed the bare wooden staircase to her

bedroom. The old worn carpet had long since been thrown out, but the new one that had been promised had never materialised.

She examined herself in the mirror. Jane Nicol, sixteen, slim, good figure, 'drop-dead gorgeous – I wish!' At least she managed a smile. Her brown hair, medium length and cut in a fashionable straggly style, brought out her light brown eyes, which many said were her best feature. She was wearing a white, printed T-shirt, cut high near the shoulders, which she liked as it showed off her fit, tanned arms. Light blue shorts and trainers completed her outfit. She took a beige, zip-up knitted jacket from her wardrobe (which contained little more than her school uniform) in case the air turned cooler.

Although Glasgow was in the middle of a September heatwave, Jane shivered when she walked out into the early afternoon air. She tried not to look at her surroundings. They depressed her. Only a few of the grim semi-detached houses were left in Morton Street. The area had been bulldozed eighteen months ago, as most of the residents had upped sticks and moved out to other parts of the city, to escape the drug dealing, violence and other crimes. The few houses that remained, like a cancerous growth on the flesh of the city, were occupied by people who had given up the ghost. They simply didn't care any more.

What bothered Jane more than anything was that she knew there had been a time when her dad had led a pretty good life. She had pieced together the various strands of her parents' story from things they had told her and from friends and neighbours. Hughie Nicol had lived in the south side of the city all his life. He had been a session musician, playing guitar in recording studios with many of the big stars. He had often worked in the BBC studios in Queen Margaret Drive.

Through the BBC he had met, and married, Rona, who was carving out a very nice career for herself as a marketing executive. They had two children – Barry and, two years later, Jane.

Then it all started to go horribly wrong.

At first the coke was purely for fun. Doing a line helped tensions melt away after work. Most people they knew were into it. It was the 'done thing' at the parties they attended. And they were mature, sophisticated adults – they could handle it . . .

Rona was the first to change. She became irritable, anxious, and more and more money was dedicated to chasing the white dragon that was taking over her life.

Then one night, when Jane was almost twelve and Barry fourteen, Hughie came home from a late-night session and found his wife lying curled up snug on the carpet, like her two children upstairs in bed. But Rona was dead.

The coroner called it a 'cocaine-induced cardiac arrhythmia'. Later, Jane made enquiries and found out what this meant: the cocaine had caused irregular heartbeats, leading to cardiac arrest and sudden death. It was more common than people realised.

Hughie never recovered. He struggled valiantly for a couple of years, but couldn't really cope. He was of a generation who were used to having the women in their lives take care of the whole domestic bit. He lost his job, and when he could no longer afford the cocaine, he succumbed to the false promises of heroin, which he bought from street dealers instead. He lost his nice home in Bellahouston and moved back to Morton Street where he'd grown up.

Jane shivered again. She made her way into Broomloan Road and headed south towards the massive red-brick structure that was Ibrox Stadium, home of the Glasgow Rangers Football Club.

It was ironic, she thought. In the open spaces where the houses had been, life was flourishing – but it was the life of weeds, vigorously thrusting themselves upwards in joyous celebration of the sun. There were nettles and gorse bushes, dockens, grasses, all intermingling in a riotous display of greens and yellows and pinks. So why are the *people* dying off? Jane asked herself. Well, if the plants can survive here, so can I.

With that, she lifted her chin and strode purposefully towards the stadium. At Ibrox Business Park, the atmosphere changed immediately. Already cars were being parked in every conceivable nook and cranny where the new modern buildings shook hands with the older red-brick ones. Jane joined the throngs that were wending their way to the match, shepherded along by stern-faced police officers astride massive brown horses.

The big-match atmosphere never failed to grip Jane. Men, women and children of all ages, bedecked in replica football shirts, multi-coloured scarves and tall hats with red, white and blue rosettes – singing, clapping, smiling, waving their flags and banners. The snack vendors were doing a roaring trade, and the air was thick with the smell of hotdogs, greasy burgers, pizzas and popcorn. For Jane, this was preferable to the cold stench of death, which she temporarily forgot.

She crossed at the roundabout and made her way along Edmiston Drive, past the stadium. She knew exactly where she was going. Beyond her, heading towards the river and the Kingston Bridge, were the solid, four-storey, sandstone flats where the 'better-off' people lived. These houses had small lawns with trees and neatly clipped hedges.

Admiring the houses took Jane out of herself for a while, until she eventually reached a school building.

Stopping at the gates, she stood for at least five minutes and let her mind wander. She imagined parents driving up in their Saabs, 4x4 Land Rovers and Jeeps. In her mind she could hear school kids laugh and joke as they made their way to their classes, in their clean and beautifully pressed uniforms, confident and secure in their middle-class existence. More than anything, Jane longed for their advantages, for their lifestyle.

She sighed as she turned away. Birthday or not, she had the week's shopping to do. It was nice to dream, but she knew her reality.

It was a half-mile walk to the nearest Asda store, and as she strolled along Jane carefully worked out her budget. She knew by heart every special offer she was after and had her money-off coupons carefully stashed in her purse. Oh, and she had to make sure she had enough for a taxi home, as she couldn't carry all those bags herself. She'd decided to go ahead with the special meal. It was just a pity she wouldn't have enough money for even a small birthday cake. Maybe her dad and Barry were just groggy after their nights out, and they would have some prezzies for her at dinner. I'll give them the benefit of the doubt, she thought, picking a trolley and beginning her long trek round the supermarket aisles.

* * *

Jane paid the taxi-driver and lugged the plastic bags into the house. She'd hoped her dad and Barry would be there to help her unload, but both had gone out. With a practised hand she soon had the groceries neatly stacked in the kitchen cupboards and small fridge. 'Right,' she said aloud. 'Let's get this occasion under way. Happy birthday to me!'

She thought about moving the kitchen table into the living room to give more of a sense of occasion. The house was small and didn't have a separate dining room, so they usually had their meals in the kitchen. A whiff of the stale smells still pervading the living room, however, soon put paid to that idea. 'The kitchen will have to do,' she said.

She went over to the sideboard and took out the only tablecloth they had. A wave of anger surged through her as she remembered the large box of fine cutlery that used to be kept there, but which, like so many things over the years, had vanished.

Jane switched off these thoughts and returned to the task at hand. She spread the tablecloth and set three places with the kitchen cutlery. It looked so ordinary, but when she added the deep red paper napkins she had bought at Asda, even she was pleased with the effect. She mustered three glasses, and had to admit they looked much better than the chipped mugs they usually used.

To make it easier on herself, she had bought a prepared prawn cocktail as a starter, to be followed by a ready-cooked, spit-roasted chicken and a nice salad. And, of course, her favourite – Vienetta!

Half an hour later Hughie and Barry came in together from the local bookmakers. The glum looks on their faces announced that luck had not been on their side.

When Hughie saw the brightly laid kitchen table he immediately perked up. 'Weh-heh, what's all this then? Have you had a win we don't know about, pet?'

'Actually, *you* were the winner. Sixteen years ago.' Seeing the puzzled look on her dad's face, Jane became exasperated. 'Do you still not remember? Think, Dad, September?'

'Oh my God,' said Hughie. 'It's not your birthday this week, is it?'

'Yes, it is. Today even!'

Father and son stood frozen in the kitchen doorway with sheepish looks on their faces.

'Well, eh,' said Hughie, 'I was planning it for next week. I must have got my dates . . .'

'Well, not to worry,' interrupted Jane, wanting more than anything to believe him.

'Sorry – eh – Happy Birthday, Jane!' he added awkwardly.

'Oh, sit down, the pair of you. I'll be back in a minute.' Forcing herself to maintain her composure, Jane went upstairs. She was determined that all her efforts would not be ruined by a fall-out. She just wanted to remove herself from the situation, calm down, then go back to them. She went into the bathroom and stared at herself for a few moments in the mirror. 'Right, Jane Nicol, sixteen,' she said. 'Things can't go on as they are. You've got to do something . . . But what?'

Although it was the last thing she felt like doing, Jane smiled and made her way back to the kitchen.

Chapter 1

At 8:35 on Monday morning the Underground Station at Hillhead in the north side of the city was disgorging its contents into Byres Road. It was the usual mixture of university students, office workers and school kids, in no less than three different uniforms. Even at this hour, the sun was bathing the area in warmth.

A group of five students, wearing the distinctive blue, white and grey of Hillside High School, met outside the station, then, without bothering to walk the twelve metres or so to the pedestrian crossing, picked their way across the busy two-lane road. As usual, they simply ignored the hoots of angry motorists.

'Let's stop at Greggs. I'm starving,' said Victoria, a

pleasant-faced, slightly plump girl in her Fourth Year.

'You're *always* starving,' said Nick, one of the two boys in the group.

'It's this heat,' protested Victoria, although even she couldn't see any logic in her reply. 'What about you, Mel – fancy anything? My treat.'

'Um . . . yeah, thanks. I'll have a chocolate doughnut.'

'Anyone else?' asked Victoria.

The rest shook their heads. Nick said, 'I'll get my own.' Victoria was the expansive, gregarious type, always looking after everyone – 'Mother Earth' as Raj called her – and Nick didn't like to take advantage of her.

They left the bakery and made their way up Ruthven Street to the school at the top of the hill. 'So, what were you up to at the weekend, Mel?' asked Julie. 'Anything exciting?' She sniffed and automatically applied a tissue to her nose.

'Riding the whole day Saturday,' said Mel, almost apologetically. 'The regional trials are coming up pretty soon. Is that another cold you've got?'

Julie sniffed again. 'Yeah. The doc says my immune system still hasn't adapted to Scottish bugs.' She grinned a rather toothy grin, which reminded Nick of the horses Mel was always going on about.

'How can you get so many colds in this heat?' he asked.

'You call this *heat*? Back home this would be a mild winter!' she laughed. Julie was from Sydney, Australia, and had moved here with her parents, who were researching Sports Medicine at Glasgow University on a two-year exchange. She'd settled really well into school life, despite the odd difference, like having to say 'S4' or 'Fourth Year' instead of 'Year Ten'. However, the climate change was posing a few problems.

'I know what you mean,' said Raj. 'But every time I go to India I can't wait to get back here, *away* from the heat.'

'That's because you were *born* here like the rest of us!' said Nick, thumping him on the back and smartly getting out of the way before Raj could return the compliment.

'I *love* the heat,' said Mel. 'I don't really like flying, but I love it when you leave Glasgow on a rainy day and step off the plane in Malaga or somewhere – the heat just *hits* you!'

'Yeah!' everyone agreed, except Nick. He liked Mel and knew she wasn't a snob, but he felt that sometimes she spoke too much about her advantages in life.

By now the group was well on its way up the hill, perspiring lightly under the weight of their heavy school bags. They'd all left their dark blue blazers at home, and were wearing the standard grey trousers or skirts, open-necked white shirts, with their blue, purple and white striped ties knotted about fifteen centimetres below the neckline. Mrs McLaren, the Assistant Head, had long ago given up trying to make them 'treat the uniform with respect and tighten up those ties!'

Mel led the way. 'Come on, you lot,' she laughed. 'You can do it!'

'It's all right for you, Mel,' said Nick. 'We've had to suffer this hill for four years now.'

'Then you should be fitter than me!' Mel noticed a slightly exasperated look on Nick's face. 'Yeah, I admit this hill is a pain.' She paused. 'My dad used to run me to the gates at my last school, but it's too far for him to do that now.' Unlike the majority of Hillside students, Mel had to travel into the city from Stewarton every morning. It was a bit of a bind, but her parents had thought it worthwhile to make a placing request for her, as Hillside High School had a great reputation, not just in the academic subjects, but in sports, public speaking, art, music and so on. Although she was a relative newcomer, Mel quickly got to know everyone and was very popular.

As usual, they took their time passing Athole Gardens, a compact yet spacious public park in the centre of the avenue, which swept up and around in a circle. Mel loved to watch the grey squirrels leap and bob among the branches that bordered all the perfectly manicured lawns. Always at this time of year the flowerbeds were riotous with colour. Some elderly residents were already sitting on the benches, enjoying the sun, while others were walking their dogs around the black tarmac paths. The small iron railings that surrounded the Gardens were well maintained and painted shiny black. Together with the decorative Victorian gas lamps, perched on pillars at each corner, they gave the place an air of peace and prosperity.

'Uh-oh, don't look now, folks, but Mel's in one of her *dwams*,' said Nick, in a stage whisper that was intentionally too loud to be ignored.

'Over to you, Victoria,' said Julie.

'Yeah,' said Raj, 'get your crystals in gear!'

Mel, suddenly pale, had stopped and was gazing at the Gardens with a faraway look on her face.

'Take it easy, Mel,' said Victoria gently. 'Now. Tell me. What *exactly* is it you're seeing? Mel! Mel!'

Mel was aware that she was still next to Athole Gardens, but the voices of her friends seemed strangely distant. Gradually, her friends themselves seemed distant, and frozen in time. Some strange force was pulling Mel deep into her own mind, away from the outside world. She was powerless to resist; she was drawn deeper and deeper, until it was as if she had become a disembodied spirit who was looking in on a new life that was opening out in front of her.

The front door burst open, as though a heavy goods van from the nearby motorway had somehow lost its way and charged up the path into Jane's house. Jane was roused from a dream of two weeks spent in the Maldives, which the presenter of the holiday programme flickering in the corner seemed to think was well within everyone's budget. She instinctively knew what had caused the commotion.

'Jane!' called a distressed female voice. 'We need you. Quick!'

In the hallway, Jane was confronted by her brother, who staggered in, supported on the arms of his girlfriend, Sara. Barry looked even more pale and drawn than usual. His long, slicked-back, dark hair was dripping with blood and his bruised right ear was at least twice its normal size. His earlobe was ripped, and the gold earring he always wore was now painfully embedded in the mess. His grey Kappa T-shirt was also drenched in blood. Some of the blood had made its way on to Sara's faded denim jacket. Jane stared for a moment, contemplating her next move.

Sara propped Barry up against the wall. 'Whitey's mob again. We were a bit short of cash . . . If you think we look bad, you should see them!' Sara grinned, pushing back her dyed blonde hair from her plump, rather harsh face. Her face could have been pretty, thought Jane, in another time, another place. Jane noticed that the four large rings which were welded together with the letters S, A, R and A on Sara's right hand were also smattered in blood. Whether it was Barry's or someone else's, she didn't know.

'Into the kitchen,' said Jane, immediately taking charge. She sat Barry on a chair, ignoring his groans as she gently removed his T-shirt. She gasped as she saw two glowering, purple-black bruises on his ribcage. Clearly he had had a none-too-friendly encounter with someone's boot.

'I swear to God, Barry, you're going to get yourselves killed. Sara can do what she likes, but –'

'Hey, just a minute!' said Sara, peeved.

But by now Jane was on her high horse. 'Face it, Sara. You're not good for each other. You just pull each other down and God knows where it will all end!'

'Calm down, Jane, calm down,' muttered Barry, whose upper lip was now in a contest with his ear to see which could swell up most.

Jane turned from Sara to look at him. 'You'd better get along to the Southern. That ear might need stitches and you could have a couple of broken ribs. I'll call you a taxi so you don't meet Whitey again.'

* * *

Ten minutes later, the taxi pulled up in front of their sparse front 'garden'.

'The Southern General Hospital, please – and keep the change out of this,' said Jane to the driver, handing over some money. She didn't trust Barry with cash, and she trusted Sara even less. She knew it would only find its way to their next fix.

'Are you not coming?' asked Barry.

'No, I've had enough. It's time to stand on your own two feet, Barry.' Jane looked pointedly at Sara, who huffed in the corner of the cab, playing with the cheap 'gold' bangles that seemed to drip from her wrist. The cab quickly made its way out of the street. Like a bat out of hell! thought Jane.

Victoria was shaking Mel's shoulder, but getting no response. She glanced back at the others who were all looking on in a stunned silence. Suddenly Mel blinked and her body quivered slightly as she came back to normal. 'S–sorry . . . It was nothing!'

'No!' cried Victoria. 'Don't pretend, Mel! Hang in there. Let it *flow* through you. There's some type of energy here and you're tapping into it.' She gently rubbed the bracelet studded with crystals that she wore on her left wrist. She was very much 'into' crystal therapy and believed that the crystals, gems and semi-precious stones in her bracelet vibrated with the Earth's elements. 'All material is just a mass of vibrating energy,' she went on. 'Some people are more sensitive to it than others. You're obviously one of them, Mel. Someone – or something – is trying to contact you.'

'She's scared,' interrupted Julie. 'Maybe we should . . .'

'No!' snapped Victoria impatiently. 'Whatever it is, it's happening more and more, just at this spot.'

'But why *here?*' asked Raj.

'That's just what I want to find out,' said Victoria. Turning back to Mel, she said, 'It's not necessarily bad, Mel. Try not to fear the unknown. We've *got* to get to the bottom of this.'

'I'm fine. I just like looking at things. Don't take it all so seriously, Victoria!'

'Maybe you're right. But maybe, just *maybe*, there's something . . . I don't know . . . something ancient and elemental at this point. I think we should go in after school and see what the crystals tell us.'

'Good idea! Let's go in and have a *séance* in the middle of a park, in the middle of the day, in the middle of a heatwave. *Dead* spooky!' said Nick.

'No need to be sarcastic,' said Victoria. '*There are more things in heaven and Earth, Horatio,/Than are dreamt of in your Philosophy.*'

Nick groaned and Julie grinned. Nick staggered

about, pretending to be stabbed through the heart. 'She always *kills* me with Shakespeare.'

Victoria was quietly enjoying her victory, giving Mel time to pull herself together. She felt slightly dizzy. Her heart was thumping in her chest and her mouth was dry. 'Come on, we'll be late!' she managed to say at last. And with that, she crossed over to the road that branched off the avenue and led up to the leafy school grounds.

Chapter 2

The following day, at 8:55 precisely, the bell in the school corridor started shrieking, and Nick, who just happened to be standing under the bell in the rather narrow and confined Administration Block, almost jumped out of his shoes.

'Relax, Nick,' laughed Raj. 'Next time you'll be clawing the ceiling like a cat!'

'Why am I *always* in the wrong place at the wrong time?' Nick complained.

'Chill, *carissimo*! You're so tense,' said another friend, Angelo, giving his shoulders a mock massage.

'Geroff!' grunted Nick. 'People might start talking!'

'Look at him! So many hang-ups. You'd never guess

his mum was the school shrink. Maybe we should make an appointment for him,' joked Raj.

'She's not a *shrink*,' said Nick defensively. 'She's the school's *educational psychologist*. And I *don't* need that kind of help from her, thank you very much!' Just then, Nick relaxed, even smiled. 'I guess it's Victoria and Mel. Did you hear them yesterday? Victoria went on and on with her psychic drivel and Mel was acting like a space cadet. Sometimes I worry about her. She talks like everything's brilliant and she's probably the richest kid in the school – yet obviously something's not right.'

'What exactly happened yesterday?' asked Angelo.

'Mel had another of her trances, but this one was mega!' said Raj and proceeded to tell Angelo all about it.

'Strange,' said Angelo. 'Mel's usually good for a laugh. Wonder what's going on . . .'

'Me too,' said Raj. 'Normally she seems happy enough. She gets everyone going, doesn't she? You've got to admit, the place is a lot less boring since she came. But recently . . .'

'Who knows?' Angelo lowered his voice in mock seriousness. 'Maybe Mel and Victoria are teenage witches!'

'I don't buy that stuff, but I have to admit – they got me spooked!' said Nick.

'Yep! There's more stuff in heaven and earth... What was that line again, Horatio?' asked Raj.

Nick grinned and playfully swung his bag at Raj, before another ear-splitting sound rent the air. This time it was Mrs McLaren. 'Will you boys get out of the corridor! At your desks by nine o'clock, remember?'

'Yes, Mrs McLaren! We love you, Mrs McLaren!' chanted both boys. Just loudly enough to hear each other, but quietly enough to ensure it didn't reach her ears.

In the meantime Mel, Victoria and Julie were heading along another corridor. 'Come on,' sniffed Julie. 'We'll be late for Home Room.'

'Home Room?' The other two looked at each other and laughed. 'How often do we have to tell you? It's *Registration*!' said Victoria.

'Whatever!'

They reached the room and plonked themselves down just as the bell was ringing. 'Don't think I didn't see you heading up Observatory Road this morning,' said Victoria quietly to Mel. 'You deliberately came that way to avoid Athole Gardens, didn't you?'

'No, no,' laughed Mel. 'I just followed my nose, that's all. One way's as good as the other. But I'm feeling a lot better today.'

'Glad to hear it,' said Julie, turning round from the desk in front. 'I wish *I* was. The more work we get at school, the worse my cold seems to get!'

Mel laughed. 'What about you, Victoria? You don't look as if you're on top form today either – anything the matter?'

'Sorry,' said Victoria. 'Only I met Lisa on the way up this morning. She went on and on about how hard the exams are going to be.'

'Now there's a surprise,' smiled Mel. 'You know Lisa's the resident Prophet of Doom. You shouldn't take her seriously.'

'I know, but I *am* beginning to get a bit worried. And she just makes it worse.'

'Look, why don't we go out at lunch-time?' suggested Mel. 'We could take our packed lunches and enjoy the sun.'

'Good idea!' said Victoria. 'It'll cheer us up.'

'If we're quick off the mark we could go down to the Botanic Gardens,' said Mel.

'Brill!' said Julie. 'And if I close my eyes I might even be able to pretend we've got some *real* sunshine!'

When the lunch bell rang at one o'clock, it seemed that half the school had the same idea. Wave after wave of students headed along the driveway, flanked by the two-storey school building on one side and a line of trees and flowers on the other, which separated the drive from the playground. Beyond the school gates, everybody headed down Observatory Road towards the Botanic Gardens.

Mel and Julie, however, were not among them. They were still standing at the main entrance, waiting for Victoria. It wasn't like her to be late. 'What on earth's keeping her?' wondered Julie.

'I expect she'll be here any minute. She won't have forgotten.'

Julie decided to change the subject. She always enjoyed hearing about Mel's very full and active life. 'So, how's your local Drama Club doing, then?'

'Oh, it's great,' replied Mel, brightening. 'My mum thinks I should ease off a bit, as exams are coming up, but I keep telling her it helps me cope with all the school pressures. I'm not sure yet, but I *might* audition for the part of Sandra Dee in *Grease* after Christmas.'

'Wow! Cool! Wish they'd do shows like that at school. It's always the heavy stuff here, isn't it?' said Julie. 'I'd love to come and see you in that one.'

'I'm sure that could be arranged. *If* it comes off and *if* I get the part. Remember, though, I live miles away . . .'

Their conversation was interrupted by the arrival of a breathless Victoria. 'Sorry, you guys! The Dragon kept me behind to go over my critical essay. I told her you were waiting, but she was pleased with it, which meant it took longer!'

'That's OK,' said Mel, 'but I don't think we can make it down to the park now.'

'Yeah, sorry about that,' said Victoria. 'Why don't we just go along to Athole Gardens and sit on a bench?'

'You know we're not supposed to go in there – we're not residents,' said Julie.

'I know, but the gate's always open and we can leave if they make us. But I don't think they'll mind when they see we're the *crème de la crème* of Glasgow's youth!' Victoria made one of her Shakespearean gestures.

'Wait a minute!' said Mel, suddenly suspicious. 'You haven't engineered all this just to get me into the Gardens, have you? I told you yesterday . . .'

'No, Mel, I swear. The Dragon did keep me back. *You* would probably call it a coincidence, but I think this was *meant* to happen.'

Julie was intrigued. 'Oh, come on, Mel. If anything happens we'll *wheech* you out, double quick!' She loved using Glaswegian slang whenever she could.

'Oh, all right,' said Mel, amused. 'As I said, I'm feeling a lot better today.'

Chapter 3

Despite the sunshine, the Gardens were almost empty, and no one seemed to pay any attention to the three schoolgirls who trudged along looking for a bench that was not too shaded. 'I love these lights,' said Mel, looking down at the little baton lamps that were set into the ground on either side of the path every ten metres or so.

'Yeah, I'd love to see them at night,' said Victoria. 'Bet they look like a miniature runway.'

'No, we're *not* coming back at night – don't even think about it!' Mel said, smiling.

'Talking about runways, are either of you going away anywhere during the Christmas hols?' asked Julie.

'Well, my parents are talking about Val d'Isère for the skiing,' said Mel. 'What about you?'

'Oh, we'll probably see a bit more of Edinburgh or the Highlands.'

'I'm strictly a home bird at Christmas,' said Victoria. 'Feet up, DVDs, Thornton's Continentals. Mmm!'

The three girls spread themselves and their lunches out on a long bench, and sat happily munching in silence for a few minutes. The sky above was azure blue and cloudless, and Mel watched a Boeing 757 as it roared over them, probably off to some sunny holiday destination.

'Right, Victoria. Let's get this over with. Why were you so keen to get me here? Don't say you weren't!'

Victoria put her apple back into her plastic lunchbox before replying. 'Well . . . You have to agree, Mel, there's *something* that seems to grab you when you pass these Gardens. I wouldn't think anything of it – I see strange things all the time – it's just that you get distressed. And I want to help.'

'We *are* your friends, after all,' said Julie in support.

'I know, I know. But it's not anything I can put my finger on. I don't know why it happens just here. It's a sort of *shiver*, that's all,' Mel said, deliberately trying to play it down.

'Why don't you put on my bracelet?' said Victoria.

'There's some kind of energy at work here, and the crystals will help to channel it. You're only scared because you don't *know* what it is. Channel it through the bracelet and it might all become clear.'

Mel put her hand on Victoria's wrist to prevent her taking off the bracelet. 'Thanks, Victoria. I appreciate your help, I really do. But I'm not into this stuff and I don't want to get involved . . .' Suddenly Mel quivered as though someone had just poured ice cubes down her back.

She turned away from Victoria and buried her face in her hands. Julie and Victoria could only look at each other blankly, neither of them knowing what to do next.

Mel felt herself being drawn away from her present reality again, and every attempt to resist resulted in confusion. She felt the hands on her face, but were they her hands? She felt strange, new emotions, but were they hers? Or did they belong to this girl, whose life was being ruthlessly superimposed on her own? Mostly Mel felt afraid. She wanted to tell this Jane to leave her alone, and she just wanted to continue her lunch with her friends. But her mind seemed unable to send instructions to her body.

Jane turned the Yale key in her front door and entered the hallway. The lingering, sickly smell of hash and stale beer almost turned her stomach. She had tried in vain to get rid of it, regularly spraying the carpets and curtains with Febreze, but no sooner would she notice some progress than Hughie would light up again, or bring his mates back 'for a few' when the pub closed.

She went into the living room, knowing without looking that her dad would be sprawled on an armchair in front of the telly. 'I collected your benefit on the way home,' she said.

No answer.

'Dad!'

'Eh? Oh, aye. Leave it on the sideboard, darlin.' He never even looked in her direction, but this did not surprise her. She looked around at her sparse surroundings – guitar lying on a threadbare settee; wall posters proclaiming 'Legalise Cannabis', the 'gear' stashed on a shelf next to the TV . . . All testified that Hughie's life revolved around his music and his next hit. Not his daughter.

'Dad, I've been thinking, I'll have to keep a bit more back for the housekeeping.'

Now she had Hughie's full attention. His face snapped round in her direction as if his neck had been held rigid by a huge elastic band and someone had just let go.

'What d'ye mean? We've been through all this before. I give you more than enough as it is. Am I not entitled to any pocket-money?'

Not the way you spend it, Jane thought to herself. 'You should come with me to the shops now and again and you'll see just how far it goes,' she said instead.

'But there's Barry's benefit as well,' said Hughie.

Jane snorted. 'Ha! When do you think I last saw any of that?'

'OK. I'll have a word with him. Don't worry, sweetheart, it'll all work out.'

Jane turned away in disgust. It was useless to argue. Bad enough that she was expected to cook and clean for them, but trying to make ends meet was no joke. In theory they should be at least reasonably comfortable. After all, there was Hughie's unemployment benefit, his widower's allowance, Barry's unemployment, and the child benefit for Jane. Every penny that came Jane's way she accounted for and spent wisely, but the supply was drying up. How was she expected to cope? She knew that with her mother gone she had to grow up more quickly than the average teenager, but her dad and Barry were expecting far too much. She felt she was suffocating, as if the welter of bills and needs and wants was piling on top of her and slowly depriving her of breath.

'I'll have a word with him.' Jane knew from experience that either her dad would forget their conversation ever happened, or Barry would promise the earth – and then do nothing.

Jane had noticed that every so often certain items mysteriously disappeared from the house. Barry strenuously denied all knowledge, but Jane suspected that the pawnshop in Southcroft Road would tell a different story. It had been happening for a long time now. The piano was one of the first things to go after Rona's death. How Jane had loved the times she sat with her mum, exploring the keyboard and being gently introduced to the fascinating world of chords and melody. Rona had the knack of making piano lessons fun. But now the piano was gone – like so many other things.

Waste of space! she thought bitterly. In desperation she turned back to her dad. 'Dad, it's no good. There's no way I can go on running this house . . .' Her voice trailed off in mid-sentence. Hughie's eyes were closed. There was a look of cherub-like contentment on his wan face, brought on by a hash-induced stupor.

Jane turned on her heel, repulsed, then stomped out of the room and up the bare staircase. She slammed her bedroom door behind her and flung herself on her duvet, then mercilessly beat her pillow for no less than five minutes. Eventually she sat up and hugged her knees tightly to her chest.

There was a slight chill in the evening air, which reminded her that autumn weather was fast approaching and the house lacked central heating. In fact, the upstairs rooms lacked any kind of heating, which was another reason Jane was grateful for the heatwave.

On a shelf alongside her bed was Jane's pride and joy – her portable hi-fi with combined radio, CD player and tape deck. She eyed it fondly, knowing it had seen better days and was big and ugly compared to the sleek versions that were now in fashion, but she had got it for a song a couple of years back at the same pawnshop she was sure Barry was visiting.

From the bottom of her wardrobe she pulled out a large cardboard box containing all the mementoes of her mum that she had been able to gather. She rummaged for a moment, then took out an old snapshot of her mum and herself as a toddler. She gazed at it with mixed feelings. There had been so many good times – days filled with laughter, love, security . . . Jane had thought they would last forever. But then came the bad days, which became more and more frequent up until her mum's death. Her mum grew distant, less caring. Harsh words, irregular meals and the like became common. At first, Jane had blamed herself, as young children will do, believing that she had become unlovable. But in time she realised the truth. 'I almost hate myself for loving you, Mum,' she whispered. 'You should still be here, taking care of me. Not . . .' Quickly she replaced the photo, then took out a tape, which, according to her dad, had been one of her mum's favourites.

Jane carefully placed the tape, which she kept permanently spooled to Side B, in the deck and pressed PLAY.

The steely voice of Gloria Gaynor sang unaccompanied for a few bars, then was joined by her typical seventies backing group. Jane instinctively moved with the rhythm and sang along with every word.

'At first I was afraid
I was petrified . . .'

Her voice grew stronger. She sometimes wondered if her dad heard her singing, but if he did it was never mentioned.

'Did you think I'd lay down and die?
Oh no, not I,
I will survive.
For as long as I know how to love
I know I'll stay alive...'

When the song ended, Jane stood, alone and lonely, tears flowing down her cheeks.

Mel was brought back to reality by a tug on her arm. 'What did you feel, Mel?' asked Victoria doggedly.

'Just leave it,' Mel said. Her voice was childlike and muted. Her mouth was dry again and her heart was thumping. 'Just let it go. I'm fine.' She didn't feel like discussing it. These visions were coming to her more and more often recently, and each time she was filled with a sense of fear, mixed with sadness and guilt. She couldn't think of any way to explain to her friends what was happening and wasn't sure she wanted them to know. She let out a shiver.

'My gran used to say that happened when someone was walking over your grave,' whispered Julie.

'Well, we usually say it's an angel passing,' Victoria said, smiling. 'That's much more pleasant.'

'Come on, Mel, enough for today,' said Julie. 'Isn't it time we were getting back anyway? What do you say to a Starbucks after school?'

'Great idea,' said Mel, gathering her lunch things together. The last thing she felt like right now was food. 'But I'm going to the Homework Club first. I want to get everything out of the way, so I can have more time later on.'

'OK, why don't we all go? I suppose we could all use it. But then it's down the hill for a large latté and a double chocolate-chip cookie. I'll have earned it by then. And don't worry, Mel, whatever it is, we'll get it sorted,' Victoria promised.

Chapter 4

'Just as well we've got PE this afternoon,' said Victoria, trying to make herself heard above the noise in the vast Games Hall that housed the fitness equipment and the games courts. 'It'll give me a chance to work off the calories I'm going to put on at Starbucks.'

Julie laughed. 'Only you would think about losing weight before you actually put it on!'

'It's all about balance,' replied Victoria. 'A couple of sessions on the treadmill and the exercise bike, and I'll *need* something to stop me fading away to a shadow.'

They made their way along the side of the playing courts to the back of the hall where the exercise equipment was stationed. They were among the first to get there, so they had their choice of machines. Victoria picked the treadmills that faced out on to the netball courts. 'It's not like you to put yourself on show,' commented Julie.

'I know, but I want to keep an eye on Mel,' replied Victoria.

The teachers considered Mel one of the leading lights in the PE Department, and had asked her to work with the younger kids. Today Mel was going to try her hand as a referee for one of the First Year netball matches.

Together Julie and Victoria keyed in their data for the treadmills. 'A five-minute warm-up walk at Level 5, I think,' said Julie, 'followed by a ten-minute run at Level 8.' The machines whirred into action and both girls began their brisk walk to keep up the pace. Julie glanced over to Victoria's console. 'Hey! Haven't you forgotten something?' she asked in mock severity. 'I don't see any *incline* on yours.'

'Trust you to notice,' groaned Victoria, pressing the incline button only as far as Level 2. 'That'll be enough, otherwise the poor machine won't take the strain.'

Julie chuckled; she loved the way Victoria didn't take herself too seriously.

Just then the First Year netball girls came running out of the changing rooms. There were two teams of seven, one team with red bibs, the other with green, tied over their PE kits. All had position letters on the front and back of the bibs: GS for Goal Shooter, WA for Wing Attack and so on. They were followed by the teacher and by Mel, who wore a grey tracksuit and had a whistle round her neck and a stopwatch in her hand.

Victoria whistled softly. 'Look at her!'

Julie cast a sideways glance. 'You're not jealous, are you?'

'Not at all!' Victoria replied with obvious sincerity. 'I admire her. I could never do that in a thousand years. I know my limitations! I just hope it's not all going to go pear-shaped, that's all.'

'Do you really think it's something serious? Do you think Mel's cracking up?'

'I don't know. But there's something influencing her right now – and that could *make* her crack up.'

Both girls watched in silence as Mel, despite their concerns, displayed all the confidence and skill of a professional. The game flowed freely, and when Mel spoke, it was in a friendly yet authoritative tone – one that commanded respect from the juniors. Victoria and Julie could hear her calls clearly.

'Shots can only be taken within the goal circle, remember!'

'You can't hold the ball for more than three seconds – keep it moving. That's it!'

'No, no, Goal Attack, you've taken more than two steps with the ball!'

'Well played, Reds!'

Before long the first quarter was over and there was a three-minute interval. While the girls changed ends, Mel stood at the side.

'Look, look!' said Victoria to Julie. They tensed as they watched Mel for signs that she was having another of her spells.

But just then, Mel glanced over at them and waved, treating them to a wide, happy grin.

Both girls relaxed visibly. 'OK, don't let's get carried away, Victoria,' hissed Julie. She did her best to smile back at Mel.

After PE the three girls met up again at the Homework Club, which was held in the English Department. Mel breezed in, looking refreshed and full of life. Victoria was bedraggled and still out of puff. 'How do you do it, Mel? I am still *knackered*!'

'You know what they say, Victoria. No pain, no gain! Keep going *regularly*, that's the secret.'

Victoria plonked herself at a desk and settled down to work. 'I just hope I've enough energy to work on this History assignment.'

About forty-five minutes later Mel got up and

crossed over to Victoria's desk. 'Victoria, I'm fine. Really!'

'What do you mean?' asked Victoria, trying to sound puzzled.

'Don't think I haven't noticed you watching me like a hawk. You've been at it since we came in!'

'It's just that there's something going on, Mel. I know there is, and you'll not let me help. The crystals can help, you know. Give them a chance.'

'We'll see, Victoria, we'll see. But right now I'm fine. Honest!' Mel sat down again, but Victoria couldn't help noticing the crease on her friend's brow, and despite her tanned features there was a paleness in her complexion that suggested all was not as well as she pretended.

Chapter 5

Mellow yellow! That was the phrase that always came to mind when Mel emerged from Ruthven Street in to Byres Road. She tended to remember places by their colours rather than by their shapes or sizes. Yellow was definitely the colour for this place. Right across the road was a bright yellow pub called The Curlers, and squeezed in between it and the brown-brick Underground station was a Starbucks coffee shop. No wonder I nearly missed it the first time! thought Mel. It was yellow too.

Mel, Victoria and Julie made their way inside, and Mel smiled as she noted the yellow walls, small circular yellow tables, light pine chairs, and yellow shades on the small wall lamps – not at all like the usual greens and browns you see in Starbucks. They walked through to the back of the café, where the large square floor tiles gave way to a more intimate section with laminate flooring and small modern art prints on the walls.

They were instantly greeted by Nick, Angelo and Raj, tucked in a corner on a three-seater mustard settee across from two large armchairs – one brown, the other a mottled green. They had come down a little earlier, because as usual, they'd opted not to go to the Homework Club.

'Just like you lot to grab all the soft seats!' said Mel.

'We never saw you at the Homework Club,' said Victoria.

'No, we didn't make it,' replied Nick. He clicked his fingers rhythmically and sang: 'It's too darn hot! Too darn hot!'

'Belt up, Nick!' said Julie. 'You're not on stage now.'

'Sit down, *bellissima*,' said Angelo. 'It's never too hot for a *cappuccino*.' Although he was second-generation Italian and spoke with a Glaswegian accent, Angelo always liked to throw in the odd Italian word and pronounce it with a full-bodied Italian accent. The girls had interrupted a heated discussion about whether there were more Italian or Indian restaurants in Glasgow.

The girls settled down and were soon caught up in

the banter. Good to see Mel relaxing, Victoria thought to herself. As time passed, she kept a watchful eye on her friend. At one stage she had to smile in between mouthfuls of her double chocolate-chip cookie. 'She's my best friend, but she tries *so hard* to impress everyone!' Mel was desperately applying a damp tissue to a coffee drip on her pristine white school shirt. She hadn't noticed the unsightly dribble of brown coffee that ran down the side of her mug. Victoria also noticed the attention Mel was receiving from Nick. I think our Nick's taking quite a shine to Mel, she noted inwardly.

The truth was that Nick, too, had noticed the changes that were taking place in Mel and was becoming more concerned. He would never admit it, even to himself, but he *was* attracted to her and felt an overwhelming desire to protect her. There was a sensitivity, a vulnerability about Mel that he just couldn't ignore, despite all her talk. And he saw Victoria as a threat. Nick didn't go in for all that astral mumbo-jumbo. It scared him, but, again, he would never admit that either. Victoria must not be allowed to drag Mel into her way of thinking. Mel was the active type, after all. She was the type who needed to face her problems head-on, to *do* something and see concrete results. Not to sit around gazing at crystals and waiting for the stars to intervene!

Chapter 6

The school's ancient PA system crackled into life as if it, too, was reluctant to get the school day under way. There was the customary *ding-dong* that always made Mel feel she was at an airport about to hear an important message. Instead, though, it was the Dragon again. Mrs Brewster was an English teacher and the Head of Fourth Year, and her nickname was well deserved.

Her tone at this time of day, however, was quite civil: 'This is a reminder to Fourth Years that you have an assembly this morning at nine o'clock. Would all Fourth Year pupils – and their Registration teachers – make their way to the Assembly Hall now, please? Thank you.'

The PA system clicked off, and there was a loud groan in all the Fourth Year classes. 'What's this assembly for?' Julie asked of no one in particular.

Lisa, a small, intense girl with glasses and acne, answered, 'It'll be about the prelims. They're going to be so hard this year! I'm going to fail them all, I just know it.'

Mel and Victoria flashed a look of rebuke at Julie. The last thing anyone wanted was to get Lisa going.

'Don't worry,' Mel said soothingly, 'they're not for ages yet. They just want to make sure we keep on top, that's all.'

Lisa had been right about the topic of the assembly. No sooner had they taken their seats in the spacious Assembly Hall, than the Dragon mounted the steps to the stage and launched into her tirade of fire and brimstone. Mel and Victoria's eyes met and an almost indiscernible smile passed between them. Every time the Dragon took an assembly Mel was reminded of the movie *The Witches*, when a poor soul who dared to make a comment was burnt to a frazzle by the chief witch.

For twenty minutes the Dragon roared on and on about the Scottish exam system. The Preliminary Examinations would be held just before Christmas.

48

They were a 'practice run' for the end-of-session Certificate exams in June. They would give everyone – teachers, pupils and parents – an indication of progress, and the results could be used in appeals if the marks in the real exams weren't up to scratch. These exams could affect the rest of their lives, and they'd be here before they knew it; they'd better get working now or they'd regret it. Success would only come with blood, sweat and, if necessary, tears; there was no such thing as a free lunch. They'd get the grades they deserved . . .

On and on she went, and Mel could see poor Lisa wringing her hands in despair.

At the end of the assembly there were a number of ashen faces in the hall. As the students made their way to their classes in a gloomy silence, Mel turned to her friends and whispered, 'I don't think that was the best approach. I wish she'd *encourage* us more. Half the kids are terrified.'

'How about you, Mel. How do you feel?' asked Victoria.

'Oh, you know me. I'll get on with my work anyway, so all that stuff's just water off a duck's back.'

Victoria was impressed by the way her friend had applied herself since coming to Hillside, so it was no surprise Mel was one of the most promising students in the Fourth Year.

49

'How about you?' asked Mel.

'Can't help feeling a bit of the colly-wobbles!' said Victoria.

'Me too,' said Nick, and that was the signal for the floodgates to open. Everyone within ten metres started voicing their fears and anxieties about the exams.

'The trick is just to keep calm,' said Mel. 'If we can keep up to speed with the class work and assignments, the exams'll take care of themselves.'

'Suddenly the Homework Club seems a good idea,' said Nick.

'Yeah,' Raj whispered to Nick under his breath. 'Mel will be there. That should keep *you* happy!'

Nick shoved Raj and soon they were grappling each other in the narrow corridor like WWE wrestlers.

'You boys!' shrieked a familiar voice from the other end of the corridor.

'Whoops!' said Raj, as they broke up, lowered their heads and mingled subtly with the crowds.

Chapter 7

The first lesson on the timetable was Maths, and everyone was glad that at least the assembly had taken up almost half the period. The teacher, Mr Guppy – or The Fish, as he was known – gave a short lesson at the board, and then gave the pupils some work to do on their own. Everyone set to, and soon there was an industrious silence, broken only by the footsteps of The Fish as he walked around peering over their shoulders.

As Victoria struggled with her equations, she happened to glance in Mel's direction. Was she wrong, or was Mel looking as if she was having another of her spells . . . ? No, must be the light, she said to herself and got on with her work. A second glance a few moments later, however, showed that Mel clearly *was* out of sorts. Her head was lowered and she was shaking it from side to side, as if to rid herself of some nasty thought. Maybe the Dragon's got to her after all, mused Victoria.

But it was definitely not the Dragon that was bothering Mel. She normally had no trouble applying herself in Maths, but somehow today it was different and she was really struggling to concentrate. Despite her efforts, her mind kept drifting. And then she began to feel another vision coming on. Mel tried to shake her head vigorously to ward off the intrusion, but felt her head respond only in slow motion. Again there was the by now familiar feeling that she was a separate being from her body. Her resistance caved in.

Jane entered her room and went over to her open window. She breathed in the cool evening air for a minute or so, then turned around – and stopped instantly in her tracks. Her eyes were fixed on the shelf alongside her bed. The soft toys on the shelf were all in place, but there was an empty space in the middle. Jane stared at the emptiness in disbelief. The gap seemed to grow in size, until it was a gaping chasm, taunting her, mocking her. She felt her head about to burst. 'Barry!' she screamed. She raced for the stairs, almost missing a step in her rage. 'Barry!'

There was no reply. Instead, all she heard was a scarper of footsteps and the slamming of the back door.

Hughie came into the hallway, holding both hands out in an attempt to placate his daughter. 'What's up, pet, what's up?'

'It's Barry, he's nicked my hi-fi. Did you know anything about this?'

'No, darlin', I swear I didn't.'

'The bastard! I'll probably never see it again.' Something in her dad's manner made her ask, 'Are you sure you know nothing?'

'Well . . . I did ask him to pawn something from the house. Just till we get the next Giro, you understand. We're short of cash. But I never meant him to take any of your stuff, Jane, I swear to God. He'd no damn right taking it without asking you!'

Jane shook her head, desperately looking for words to express how she felt. 'Dad! Dad!' she blurted out, bursting into long, deep sobs. 'You're both as bad as each other! Can't you see what's happening?' She was shouting by now. 'Barry looks up to you. He sees you killing yourself with drink and drugs, so he just follows you like a sheep!' She was screaming, unable to control her rage. 'Some example you are to him!'

Jane stopped in full flight when she saw the blood drain from her father's face, turning it a deathly shade of pale. He

53

seemed to literally wither in front of her as his shoulders hunched and his knees bent. 'I know. I know,' he said softly. And with that, he turned, walked through to the living room and slumped into his chair.

Jane stood for a moment, staring at the empty space he left behind, unsure what to do next. By now her rage was spent, so she turned away and trudged slowly back to her room. Instinctively she reached for the cardboard box in her wardrobe and took out her Gloria Gaynor tape. Only then did she remember she had nothing to play it on. She felt tears welling up again as she stood still and started to sing: 'I will survive . . .' But her voice faltered, broke off, and she flopped on to her bed and wept.

The vision of Jane vanished, and all Mel could hear was a voice in her head: 'Little Miss Rich Kid, you've got it made, you and your horse riding. Well, I want your life!'

'Leave me. I don't want this!' Mel mouthed the words, but no sound came out. Her throat was dry, her palms were sweating and she felt that horrible thumping in her chest.

'Sir! Sir!' called out Victoria. 'Mr Guppy, Mel's not well.' Without waiting for the teacher to respond, she got up, walked over to her friend and put a comforting arm around her.

'All right, no need to panic,' said Mr Guppy. The

fact that no one *was* panicking seemed irrelevant to him. 'What's up, Melissa? Are you able to walk?'

'Yes, sir. I think it must be the heat.'

'Right! Take her out for some fresh air, Victoria, and get her a drink of water. If she still feels unwell take her to the nurse. Are you both in the same class next period?'

'Yes, sir.'

'Who else is?' He turned to Julie who had raised her hand. 'Explain the situation to the teacher, will you, Julie?' Then, turning back to face Victoria and Mel, he said, 'Right, off you go.'

The pair walked downstairs in silence and went out on to the patio area at the back of the school. It was a large area, surrounded on three sides by the main block of the school and its two wings, and on the fourth side was a wooded and shrubbed area that stretched for about half an acre before meeting the private houses that backed on to it.

On the patio were picnic benches, bolted into the concrete, and large pots containing small trees and flowering plants. Mel often thought of this as a haven in the middle of the busy city. The two friends sat at one of the tables and Mel sipped from the bottled water she always carried in her bag.

'You were talking to someone, weren't you?' asked Victoria.

'How did you know?' Mel was awestruck. 'Are you *really* psychic?'

'Probably,' replied Victoria. 'But I saw your lips moving!'

Both girls burst out laughing, and the tension broke. 'Why don't you trust me, Mel? A problem halved is a problem . . . Oh gosh, I always get that one wrong!'

'I'll tell you anyway,' said Mel. 'It's happened a few times now, you were right . . .' She told Victoria all about the episodes she had recently started having – how she forgot who she was or where she was, and instead she saw the life of this other girl as though it were passing before her eyes.

But then she stopped. That was as much as she was prepared to divulge at the moment.

Mel and Victoria sat for a few moments in silence. Then Victoria was the first to speak. 'Do you know what? Don't laugh, Mel, but I think someone from the other side could be trying to contact you.'

'Victoria, get a life!'

'No, seriously, there are lots of recorded cases like this. Maybe someone, a girl of about our age, had something unfinished before she passed over. Is there anyone in your family, a cousin or someone?'

'No. I don't believe any of this for a minute! I wasn't

getting a message, anyway. This girl just wanted to . . . well, take over.'

'Ah!' said Victoria wisely. 'That's what I was afraid of. Do you know what a *Doppelgänger* is?'

'No.'

'Well, it's a German word and it literally means a 'double-goer'. It's someone who's very like you, like a twin. But maybe this is an evil one. A menacing one, alive . . . or . . . or *dead*. It can take on a ghostly form.'

'Stop it, Victoria, I don't like this!'

'Sorry, Mel. Of course you don't. But you must agree, we have to get to the bottom of it. There's got to be a reason. Maybe something horrible happened to this girl. She could be crying out to you for justice to be done. Or maybe it hasn't happened yet! You could be the key to saving her life.'

'I doubt it very much.'

'There is, of course, another possibility.'

'What?'

'Well . . .' Victoria paused. 'Mel, I'm only saying this for your own good. I don't want to scare you, but it's always better to act *before* it happens . . .'

'*What?*' Mel was almost breathless. All this talk was making her nervous.

'Maybe you're in danger of being possessed by another spirit. Someone who was very unhappy in this

57

life and can't pass over to the other side. So they're feeling lonely and desperate, and they're trying to make their existence more bearable . . .'

Mel stood up. 'Let's get back to class now.'

'OK, but Mel, you've got to face this. Time could be vital . . .'

Mel had hoped that she would eventually be able to tell her friend everything. Now she was not so sure if Victoria was the best person to help her. She *wanted* to talk, but what could she say? These episodes were not only scaring her, she was losing the plot fast. Only the other day she'd turned up in the History department when she should have been in an English class – and when she eventually made it to English, she'd forgotten to collect her books from her locker! Why couldn't she concentrate? It was no fun being a bundle of nerves all the time, worrying about when the next 'episode' would come. She knew that Victoria was only trying to help. But how could she tell her everything when she would just turn it into something ghostly and horrific?

Chapter 8

The following morning at 10:55, the bell rang, indicating the start of the morning interval. Mel and one of her classmates, Gordon, moved swiftly along the corridor to the Social Area, just outside the Assembly Hall. It was here that Molly, one of the school auxiliaries, set up the tuck shop every morning.

'Thanks for reminding me, Gordon. Molly won't be too pleased,' said Mel.

'No bother,' replied Gordon, a tall, lanky lad with short, fair hair. 'It's not like you to forget, though. We nearly both forgot today!' It was the custom for the Fourth Year prefects to take turns helping at the tuck shop, and they were permitted to leave class a few minutes before the bell to get there on time.

'Hello, you two. Better late than never! I thought I'd been abandoned today,' said Molly. Mel was pleased to see the smile on her face. Molly was a pleasant, middle-aged Irish woman who had so many duties that many people said *she* ran the school, not the head teacher!

'Sorry, Molly!' Mel slipped in behind the long trestle table and went into action immediately. She knew by heart the price of each item and which were the favourites. When she was on duty she made a point of giving the bowls of fruit and packets of nuts a more prominent display, in an attempt to persuade people to eat more healthily. Today, though, she would just have to put up with the bars of chocolate and chewy sweets being at the front.

Molly, Gordon and Mel made a great team, and soon the long queue was moving quickly. While Mel was busy serving a group of Third Year girls, she overheard a snippet of conversation from some First Years behind them. 'Did you hear about the ghost in Room B7?' said one of the boys.

'Where's Room B7?' asked his friend, intrigued.

'You don't know? It's that one in the basement under the gym. You go down that spooky little staircase to get to it. A teacher was murdered there years ago and her body was never found. Two Fifth Years say they heard weird noises and saw this black figure . . .'

'That's enough of that!' shouted Mel. The two boys looked at her quizzically. They'd never seen Mel uptight before. 'Come on, you two, what would you like?' she added, trying to regain her composure.

The two lads bought their sweets and moved away, giggling as they went. Just then two of the Third Year girls whom Mel had served just before, came back to the front of the queue. 'Sorry, Mel,' said one, 'but you've short-changed us. We both bought the same, remember? We should have got 50p back, not 20.' Mel became flustered. Both Molly and Mel knew these girls, and they were definitely not the type to try it on.

'Don't worry, Mel, just sort it out,' said Molly.

'Sorry, girls. Here you are,' said Mel, handing over the correct change. She was conscious of Gordon smirking behind her back. She tried desperately not to blush, especially since she now saw that Nick was in the queue. She'd been so preoccupied that she hadn't even noticed.

When the tuck shop was being cleared away Nick came back over to them. 'Hi there,' he said. 'What was that all about, then?'

'It was nothing,' said Mel hurriedly. 'Nosey!' she added, trying to smile.

But Gordon made the most of the situation. 'Oh, she short-changed some kids and got a bit embarrassed, that's all. Don't worry, she'll recover!'

Nick looked at Mel, who was blushing furiously now. He immediately wished he'd kept out of it. He smiled to her and shrugged his shoulders sympathetically, as if to say, 'Forget it, it's nothing'.

Gordon, however, blustered on. 'Actually, I have to admit I'm pleased,' he said. 'I always feel intimidated working with Mel. She's hyper-efficient at everything.' He turned and grinned at her. 'It's good to know you're human after all!'

'Thanks, Gordon,' said Mel. 'Thanks for nothing!' she added, laughing, then moved away to help Molly push the trolley of goodies back to the small room where they were stored.

Nick watched her go, thinking, What on earth's happening to you, Mel? He was aware of how sharp Mel usually was and how she hardly ever made mistakes. But all the same, this one was completely trivial, no big deal. So why was she upset? Odd . . . He decided there and then that, odd or not, Mel was a friend in need.

Chapter 9

That same day after lunch there was a double period of Drama. Victoria was in her element. They were rehearsing selected scenes from Shakespeare's *Macbeth*, and Victoria was playing none other than the evil heroine herself, Lady Macbeth.

'You've got to give the old girl credit,' said Victoria. 'She really knows how to create an atmosphere.'

'Yeah, I'll give her that,' said Nick, who was never too enamoured with Drama anyway, especially Shakespeare.

They cast an appreciative eye round the studio. The walls were entirely black and the shutters on the windows had been closed to cut out all light. There was a large floor space and at the back of the room was a six-tier bank of grandstand-style benches that could be folded and wheeled away as necessary. In the middle of the floor, the 'old girl' in question, Ms Morgan, the Drama teacher, had cleverly created what appeared to be an open fire with a large cauldron on top. The 'flames' were no more than a combination of lights, a fan, and flickering crêpe paper, but it was quite realistic and gave the studio a ghostly and mysterious atmosphere.

'OK, witches, are we ready?' called out Ms Morgan. 'Act IV, scene i. The witches are gathered around their cauldron, cooking up a special brew to give Macbeth when he comes to consult them about his future. Now remember . . .' Her voice dropped as she deliberately tried to convey the spookiness of the scene. '. . . The feeling will be created by four things: the *spectacle* of the witches and the cauldron, the *movement* of the witches and . . . what else?'

'The *words*,' some called out.

'Good! And?'

'The *rhythm*,' they all called out in unison.

Nick glanced at Mel, who had been looking pale and unsettled ever since the episode at the tuck shop.

'Excellent! Right. Cue witches!'

Although the script called for only three witches with speaking parts, Ms Morgan had twelve girls and boys, including Mel and Julie, positioned around the cauldron. The speeches were divided up among them. The rest of the class sat on the benches as an audience. On Ms Morgan's cue, the 'witches' held hands and began to move menacingly in an anti-clockwise circle.

'Round about the cauldron go;
In the poison'd entrails throw . . .'

Individuals then called out a double line each.

'Fillet of a fenny snake,
In the cauldron boil and bake . . .'

They moved forward to drop their nasty ingredients into the cauldron.

'Eye of newt, and toe of frog,
Wool of bat, and tongue of dog . . .'

When it came to the chorus the whole class joined in.

'Double, double toil and trouble;
Fire burn and cauldron bubble.'

Ms Morgan stood at the side with a contented look on her face; the spell was winding up nicely.

It was Mel's turn to speak, but when she opened her mouth, nothing came out.

'*Finger of birth-strangled babe . . . ?*' prompted the teacher, but Mel was tongue-tied.

There were cries of 'Aw, Mel!'

'Come on!'

'You're spoiling it!'

Mel felt near to tears. 'I'm sorry, Miss. My mind's gone blank. Can I just sit this one out?'

Ms Morgan realised something must be wrong, as it was unlike Mel to opt out. 'OK, Mel. If you don't feel up to it today, have a seat and you can take part in the discussion afterwards.'

Mel gratefully left the circle and went over to the others in the audience. Nick motioned for her to join him.

'Sorry, Nick,' she said.

'No need to apologise!'

'I just don't like that line about a strangled babe.'

'Take it easy. They'll manage!'

The witches' mantra was starting up again. Mel tried to get involved, but almost immediately she was aware of a weird sensation in her hands and feet. It was like they were becoming enlarged. She felt dizzy and a wave of panic welled up. Her heart seemed to be thumping in time with the chants of '*Double, double toil and trouble*', and she sensed she was slipping away . . .

* * *

It was Saturday morning, exactly one week since her sixteenth birthday, and Jane was standing in one of the aisles in Asda talking to her friend, Ruby, who was lending a sympathetic ear.

'They've had a whole week to put things right,' Jane was saying. 'I don't ever forget their birthdays. It would be nice to feel a bit appreciated, that's all.'

'I know, love, but that's men for you. Don't wait to be appreciated. You'll be hanging around a long, long time!' Ruby stacked the last of the packets of biscuits on to the shelf and began piling the empty cardboard boxes on to her trolley. She smoothed down her green overall and got ready to move off. Ruby was in her mid-forties and had the battle-weary face of one who had seen it all before. The money supply was unreliable in her home too, but her part-time job at the supermarket gave her at least some measure of independence. 'Remember, if you fancy a wee job in here I can always have a word with the supervisor.'

'Thanks, Ruby. I would – only it's a full-time job looking after the Lord of the Manor and his heir. Then there's school . . .'

'Aye, I understand, Jane. You hang in there. And if they're getting you down, just come and see your Auntie Ruby, all right?'

'Thanks, Ruby!' Jane smiled and moved towards the checkout. She always felt better after a chat with Ruby. She

67

needed a friend and Ruby was a great support. But Jane was fully aware that was as far as it went with Ruby. She had her own problems and wasn't in a position to offer any practical help.

Jane sat back in the taxi and considered her options. Barry had been conspicuous by his absence all week. No doubt he and Sara were moving around from den to den, crashing wherever they happened to find themselves. Naturally, there was no sign of the hi-fi. Jane had gone to the pawnshop to enquire, but it wasn't there. She figured Barry had probably flogged it in one of the pubs for a tenner.

As the taxi neared Morton Street, Jane looked out the window, feeling utterly depressed. The heatwave had taken a dip, and the grey skies highlighted all that was undesirable about her surroundings. Even the weeds seemed to have lost their energy and were beginning to flop over in a tangled heap. Jane took in the rusting metal railings, some with barbed wire on top, and asked herself, What's the point? Were the railings to keep the weeds away from the public or the public away from the weeds? By the time the taxi was drawing up to her front door, Jane felt as if the walls were closing in on her. She was stifled, weary. She searched her mind for words to sum up her feelings . . .

'I want your life!' The words echoed in Mel's head. Someone was tugging at her left arm.

She felt the tug on her arm again, and turned in horror to see who it was. It was Nick – and he seemed equally horrified. 'Mel! Mel, wake up!'

She relaxed slightly as the haze surrounding her began to lift and the thumping of her heart slowed down.

'You drifted off, but it seemed as if you were suffocating. Are you OK?'

'I . . . I think so,' was all she could muster. Her mouth was so dry!

'She's giving us a break. Come on out for some fresh air.'

'I'll just get my blazer.' Mel slowly lifted herself to her feet and went over to the bank of hangers. As she picked out her own blazer, she noticed a small tea or coffee stain on the lapel. She liked all her clothes to be impeccably clean. 'How could I have missed that?' she asked aloud, and immediately began picking and fussing at it.

'Out, damned spot! out, I say!'

Victoria had come up behind her unnoticed, and was quoting one of her lines from Macbeth. 'Remember what happened to Lady Macbeth, Mel. She went mad. Sorry to put it that way, but sometimes you've got to be cruel to be kind. I don't want you going the same way. I saw you over there. We've got to exorcise this ghost.'

'Oh, forget your ghosts, Victoria!' said Nick in

exasperation. 'Look, Mel, I agree with Victoria up to a point. It's obvious there's something bugging you and it *needs* to be seen to. But in a *professional way*. Why don't I have a word with my mum? She's here to help people sort things out if they get tangled up emotionally. That's her job.'

'I don't know, Nick. I'm not a great one for that sort of thing. I prefer to sort things out on my own, privately.'

'You don't need to tell *us* about it, but talking to her will help. I'm sure of it.'

'But I don't *know* her . . .'

'Oh, come on, Mel, you don't always have to be in control!' Nick snapped and immediately regretted it. 'Sorry,' he mumbled. 'Me and my big mouth again.'

'That's all right.' Despite feeling a little angry, Mel managed a smile.

That annoyed Victoria. 'But what if there are *other* forces at work here?' she blurted out. 'What then? A school psychologist won't know anything about that. She could end up making things worse!'

Nick said nothing. He looked at Mel with a steady eye, as if to say, 'Let common sense prevail, *please*.'

Mel was keen to soothe the troubled waters. 'Look, I really appreciate you both trying to help me like this,' she said. 'Let me think it over.'

She was torn. She didn't want to admit it, but the idea of professional help was beginning to appeal to her. But she didn't want to tie herself down either – nor did she want to burden her friends with it. On the other hand, the problem was now seriously affecting her life. Nick had sussed her out – she *did* like to be in control of things, and she was losing that control rapidly. It was freaking her out. She was starting to doubt whether she could manage it on her own. But how could she take Nick's suggestion without offending her best friend?

Maybe I'm going mad, she thought. She remembered being told that mental illness could be cured more easily if treatment started early. Would it be the same with this? But what if she wasn't going mad? What if there *was* something in Victoria's theories? Could that be possible? Fear was making Mel entertain all kinds of strange thoughts. Her spirits sank even deeper.

Victoria was not for turning. 'Why don't we go over to the Psychic Centre? There are lots of people there who could help.' She looked pointedly at Nick. 'Some of them have university degrees.' Victoria firmly believed in her approach, but if she was honest with herself, it was not just Nick's disagreement that annoyed her. The words 'She's *my* best friend, not yours,' were grumbling at the back of her mind.

There was an awkward silence between the three

friends as they made their way back to the drama studio. Mel felt badly being the cause of the trouble. She knew that, reluctant as she was to accept help from an outsider, it might be the only way to resolve something she'd noticed building up over the last couple of weeks: there was a definite tension between Nick and Victoria, and it was now becoming unbearable.

Chapter 10

Raj and Nick were standing outside the Assembly Hall. Their faces were glum, despite the lively music that was blaring from the speakers inside the hall.

'Cheer up, you two! You look like a pair of gargoyles,' said Julie, arriving on the scene with Victoria.

'Yeah, why don't you stand on either side of the school gates?' quipped Victoria. 'That way you might scare off the teachers before they drive in!'

'Good thinking,' said Raj. 'That way we wouldn't have Social Ed on a Monday morning. Bor-ring!'

'So *that's* what's bothering you,' said Julie. 'Well, you should have joined the mentoring programme. You could be out and about helping the younger kids during

Social Ed time, instead of having to sit in a boring lesson. It's a lot more enjoyable.'

'Yeah?' asked Nick. 'What will you be doing during Social Ed?'

'I'm in the First Year Home Economics class. Mrs Goodwin's making ice cream with them. I'll be helping out – especially at the end when we have to eat it!'

'OK for some,' said Nick.

'No thanks – not for me. Nothing could persuade me to work with those brats,' said Raj. 'Oh! Hi, Mel. How's things?' he added when he caught sight of Mel arriving, looking a bit out of breath.

'Great, thanks. I thought I was going to be late, though. The traffic's really heavy coming into the city. What are you all talking about?'

'They're moaning because they've got Social Ed and I was telling them they could have been a bit more public spirited and joined the mentoring programme,' said Julie.

Mel smiled. 'Yeah, I'm playing the piano for a First Year Music class. It's a great way to get the week under way. No strain.'

Just then the 8:55 bell rang, and they made their way to their Registration rooms.

After Registration, Mel headed for Mr Grant's class in

the Music Department. She felt more relaxed already. She liked Mr Grant; he had been quick to spot her talent and got her playing the piano soon after she arrived at Hillside. He was laid-back, unlike some teachers, who made you feel your life depended on doing well in their subjects.

Mel poked her head round the door and caught Mr Grant's eye as he was shuffling song sheets on his desk. He broke into a broad grin. 'Ah. 'Morning, Mel. How are you?'

She smiled back. ''Morning, Sir. Very well, thanks.' This was just what she needed to get her back into the groove at school, especially after that experience in Drama class on Friday.

'I thought we'd concentrate on the Caribbean medley today, Mel. It's good fun.'

'Cool!' said Mel, sitting at the piano to the side of the teacher's desk. She loved the lilting calypso rhythms, which always made her imagine she was in an exotic land of sun, sand and surf. And with the simple chords they were so easy to play.

'Uh-oh. Here come the troops. Let's get things under way,' said Mr Grant. A horde of twenty twelve-year-olds piled in through the door, smiling and laughing. They, too, liked the atmosphere in Mr Grant's classes.

'Right. 'Morning, you lot,' he called out. 'Get

yourselves organised and I'll hand round the song sheets. Let's see if we can persuade the sun to come back and stay with us a bit longer, shall we?'

Mel was already leafing through her music – 'Jamaica Farewell', 'Island in the Sun', 'Yellow Bird', 'Linsted Market' . . . Soon teacher, singers and accompanist were working together like a well-oiled unit.

'Great stuff!' called out Mr Grant when they stopped for a break. 'What do you say we start up a steel band? Some of you could play the steel drums and maracas, and the rest of you could sing. You could all wear those bright Caribbean shirts. That would go down well at concerts, wouldn't it?'

That set the cat among the pigeons. There was a surge of enthusiasm, and it took Mr Grant and Mel quite a few minutes to settle the class again. 'Right, Mel. "Island in the Sun". That should calm us down!'

Sure enough, in no time they were all caught up in the infectious lilt. Mel was relaxing with the rhythm and could imagine another life on a beautiful Caribbean island. Gradually, though, she became aware that she was playing some wrong notes and occasionally losing the beat. More than once Mr Grant frowned in her direction. He didn't want to embarrass her in front of the kids, but eventually he had no choice but to go over to her. 'What's up, Mel? You were playing brilliantly. Are you a bit tired now?'

'No, no . . . My mind was drifting. Sorry!'

But if anything, her playing became worse and soon the class stopped, horrified to see Mel sitting on her bench, staring into space as if she had been turned into a statue.

Instead of the calypso songs, Mel could hear a man playing bluesy music on a guitar and she saw posters on a wall advocating drugs. She also heard the by now familiar voice, pleading: *'Please don't ignore me, Mel!'*

Mr Grant broke out in a sweat. He was no good in a crisis. 'Melissa, for Heaven's sake wake up. What on earth's wrong?'

The panic in his voice must have touched Mel, for she shook her head and gazed around, bewildered. 'Sorry, everyone . . . I'm not feeling too good, that's all. I need to go to the loo. Excuse me, will you?' With that she hurried out of the classroom.

She burst into tears as soon as she reached the corridor and dashed to the toilets. She headed straight for the last cubicle, slammed the door, locked it, then slumped against the wall.

Chapter 11

Jane went up to the loft and pulled down an old Puma holdall that had once belonged to Barry when he played for the school team. Opening her wardrobe, she took a moment to look at her clothes. There wasn't room for everything, so she gathered the essentials: the few leisure clothes she had, her school clothes and her toiletries. It took her only a few minutes to pack. A few more personal items were stuffed inside her schoolbag. She was ready for the road.

Hughie was still in bed, snoring off the night before. 'Sorry,' Jane whispered, more to the house than to her father. 'I hope it all works out.' With tears flowing freely down her cheeks, she closed the front door softly behind her, and set off for the nearest Underground station.

She inserted her ticket into the machine, listened to it zip through and grasped it when it came out the slot on top. The small screen lit up with the word 'Enter', and Jane struggled against the chrome metal push-barrier to get herself and her bag through in one go.

Ever since she was a little girl, Jane had loved the Underground. Every station looked the same – dark orange floor tiles, brown-brick walls, the stairway with the chrome barrier in the middle that took you deep into the innards of the city, the special, earthy aroma, the platforms, the chrome-framed advertising panels – but today she made her way down, totally oblivious to all these things. She propped herself against one of the shiny wall bars, built so that people could take the weight off their legs by half-sitting, half-perching, but not quite leaning, on the wall. She breathed deeply. She had to think clearly. Her next move was crucial.

Her thoughts were interrupted by a roar from the tunnel, heralding the arrival of the next train. She remembered how she used to feel disappointed as a child, when, after such a magnificent build-up, the train that emerged just looked like a tiny orange tube. The sliding doors puffed open and then closed behind her, and she sat wearily on the orange-brown upholstered bench that ran the length of the carriage. The train pulled into the tunnel, with a clamour of jarring, grating and jostling. It was quiet at this time on a Saturday morning, and it gave her a chance to think.

She would go to the Social Work Department in the city centre and declare herself homeless. She knew that even on a Saturday there would be a social worker on duty.

Standing at the door in front of the rather forbidding building, Jane felt her tummy doing cartwheels. Worry, sadness and despair conspired to overwhelm her. She was on the point of turning around and walking right past when a young woman, probably in her mid-twenties came up behind her.

'Hello there!' She smiled at Jane.

Jane sized her up before replying. The woman had an open, friendly smile, with gleaming white teeth, and blonde hair cut short. Not much make-up, but a silver stud in her nose. She wore a casual trouser suit and held a paper bag in one hand.

'Hi,' replied Jane.

'Have you been in to the office? I just stepped out for some supplies,' she said, indicating her paper bag.

Jane relaxed immediately. 'I haven't been in yet, but I was hoping to talk to a social worker.'

'Oh, that'll be me, then. I'm Penny.'

'Jane. Jane Nicol.'

'Come on in, Jane. I hope you like Danish pastries. I always buy too many. I think my eyes are bigger than my tummy!'

Ten minutes, a Danish and a Diet Coke later, Jane had told Penny all about life in Morton Street. 'I don't want to cause any trouble, but I need to get away to think things out, even if it's just for a while.'

'Have you no relatives who could put you up?' asked Penny.

'My mum's parents are down south, but they don't want to know us after what happened. I think they blame my dad. And his folks are dead. Apart from a sister who lives outside the city, but I honestly don't want to go to her.'

Penny thought seriously for a minute. 'Well, now you're sixteen you can, of course, leave home and live where you want. But before you can find somewhere permanent, we'll have to get you somewhere in the short term. The only possibility right now is the Hector Campbell Centre in St Vincent Street.'

'What's that?' asked Jane.

'It's a supervised accommodation for young people in your position. It used to be a hotel, but it couldn't compete with the likes of the Hilton and the Holiday Inn. It was taken over by the council a few years ago. But I warn you, it can be quite rough! Are you interested?'

'You know what they say,' replied Jane. 'Beggars can't be choosers!'

'Let me make a phone call, then.'

* * *

Jane walked along from Union Street, and for the second time that day found herself standing outside a gaunt building, wishing she wasn't there. 'Oh well. Here goes!' she said to herself and pushed her way through the revolving door.

The reception area had a garish, plastic feel to it, as if it were doing its best to be cheerful, but not succeeding. Jane noticed that the floor tiles were chipped and worn and the walls and skirting were scuffed. A placard announcing: We've seen better days! would not have been out of place. Instead there was one saying: Positively no alcohol or drugs on these premises.

A stern, matronly figure peered at Jane over the top of her glasses. 'Ye-es?'

'I'm Jane Nicol. Penny Armstrong asked me to hand in this.' She passed over a sealed manila envelope.

'Ah yes, she telephoned about you earlier. We have a room ready for you upstairs. Read this leaflet first, though. Just a few Dos and Don'ts – common sense things really.' The receptionist did her best to smile. 'Make sure you note the Fire Exits, and there must be no smoking in bed. Oh, and, er – this rule is very important!' She glared as she pointed to the placard on the wall.

'I don't smoke, I don't drink, and I certainly don't do drugs!' snapped Jane.

'Yes, well . . . Here's your key, Room 25. The cafeteria will be open from five until nine.'

Room 25 was small and narrow, and to the left there was a built-in cupboard with a flimsy curtain instead of a door. A single bed and a wooden desk and chair completed the furnishings. The toilet and shower block were along the hall.

The first thing that struck Jane about the room was the smell. A cheap disinfectant had been used to try and mask the smell of stale sweat and Heaven knows what else. She walked over to the window and slightly cheered up when she saw the view. The Centre was placed right on the brow of St Vincent Street, and she could see all the way across to the Kingston Bridge, part of an eight-lane motorway that linked the north and south of the city. Just a short trip along the motorway would take you beyond Govan, out to where they lived in Morton Street. The realisation caused her heart to become heavy again. She pictured Hughie and Barry, probably floundering without her, arguing over who should go to the local chippie because they couldn't cook for themselves. If they have any money left! she thought.

That reminded her. By now it was a quarter past five, so the cafeteria would be open. The day's events had made her hungry.

Jane hardly tasted the stodgy chips and leathery burgers that passed for the evening meal. She was too aware of the group of three young men who were leering at her from another table. The occasional obscene comment drifted over, accompanied by a burst of coarse laughter.

'Don't mind them,' said a pale young woman, who looked as if she was about twenty going on fifty-five and was about to expire any minute. 'If they try anything, just report them to the supervisor. They're animals!'

'Thanks,' said Jane. 'One of them tried it on already, but he got a flea in his ear.' She tried to smile. She was used to Barry's mates and she had learnt to fend for herself.

'Look,' said the young woman, whose black dress, sunken eyes and hollow cheeks made Jane think she looked like a relative of the Addams Family. 'If you want some company later, I can fix you up with anything you want. Know what I mean?'

'Thanks, but I'm fine,' mumbled Jane, picking up her tray and getting out of the cafeteria as quickly as she possibly could. The hoots and whistles of the boys rang in her ears. She almost ran to her room in fear and disgust. She locked the door and placed the chair at an angle against it, the way she'd seen it done in the movies, then sat on the bed and tried to take stock of her life.

Why do I feel like this? she asked herself in despair. It was a deep, deep sadness. She pressed her hands to her heart, almost literally feeling the hurt there, as if a massive bird of prey had ripped her open with its talons and was clawing at her.

Her mind was ravaged by mixed emotions about her dad.

How could she leave him on his own? He was hopeless, he was outrageous. She could easily throw herself at him and beat the living daylights out of him . . . So why do I bother? she asked herself. Deep down she knew why she bothered – she wanted to take care of him, make him realise there was life after Rona. If only he would rouse himself and make the effort.

I've got to go back, she told herself. There was no way he could survive by himself and there was no way she could live with herself if she stayed away. 'God help us,' she said aloud.

Just then she heard a commotion in the corridor. The boys from the dining room were looking for her. The obscene comments were now pouring out fast and furious and the raucous laughter was becoming louder by the minute. Jane winced as someone banged fiercely on her door. Then the handle turned, but the lock held firm. She was petrified, too scared even to scream. The ordeal continued for what seemed a lifetime, until another, adult voice was heard in the corridor. An unpleasant exchange followed, and at last the boys dispersed, grumbling and complaining among themselves. Jane feared it might be a trick and a full half hour passed before she could summon the courage to open the door slightly and peer outside.

Ten minutes later, Jane handed in her key at the desk without a word and made her way back to the Underground.

Chapter 12

Mel pulled herself together, went over to the washbasin and washed her face and hands. She dried them at the drier, then checked herself in the mirror. Outwardly she appeared calm and resolute, despite the paleness of her complexion, but inwardly her mind was a seething mass of confusion. She decided to do her tuck shop duty, then call it a day and go home early.

Mr Grant had already informed her Guidance teacher that she'd been unwell, so a pass-out was easily arranged.

On her way to the Underground at Hillhead she took a slight detour past University Avenue, which she often did when she was on her own. She loved to look right up University Avenue at the magnificent steeple of the university building, hundreds of years old, rising above the trees and imagine herself as a university student.

But this morning it was different. She stopped and took in the broad sweep of the avenue. The trees seemed to blur the view of the steeple and the incline on the avenue appeared much steeper than usual.

Well, *she* was different, she realised that much. There was heaviness in Mel's heart that was weighing her down. Why am I like this? she wondered. I'm definitely going mad. She turned in a daze into Byres Road and headed for the Underground.

Constable Linda McLean was weary and was looking forward to the end of her shift. Must be getting old, she told herself. Although she much preferred working for the British Transport Police to pounding the beat for the regular Force, the downside was that she now met many more hopeless cases, the casualties of life who were drawn to railway stations as if by a magnet.

Her practised eye narrowed its focus and zoomed in on a girl struggling up the escalator on to the main concourse of Glasgow Central Station. Linda scowled and shook her head disapprovingly. The girl looked dazed and appeared to stagger slightly. She was wearing the uniform of Hillside High School, one of the most prestigious schools in the city. Could she be drunk? Surely not! But it did warrant some investigation.

Mel was out of puff when she saw the police officer approaching her. Normally she would have been slightly alarmed, but today everything seemed to melt into one big haze. The knot of anxiety in her tummy was as tight as it had been when she left school, and what little clarity she had left was targeted in one direction: home. But what did the police want with her?

'Hello, love,' said Constable McLean. 'Everything OK, is it?'

'Y – Yes, thanks,' said Mel. She was perspiring now, and allowed her heavy schoolbag to slip from her shoulders and rest on the floor. It had been a tiring walk from the Underground to the station.

'It's just that you looked as if you might be unwell.' You had to be careful what you said to people these days, especially youngsters. Start accusing them of anything and Daddy's solicitor would be down on you like a tonne of bricks!

'No, I'm all right,' said Mel, doing her best to smile. 'I'm a bit hot, that's all.'

'A bit early to be going home, is it not? Where are

you headed, love?' Linda McLean deliberately leaned forward and bent down solicitously, but it was really to catch a whiff of Mel's breath.

'I got away early today. I'm going to catch a train home to Stewarton.'

No, no alcohol there, decided Linda. She surveyed Mel's glistening forehead, her wan face and her glazed eyes. Could be drugs, she concluded. 'Ah, that'll be Platform 12. Are you sure you're OK?'

'Yes, thanks,' said Mel, lifting her bag and pressing on towards the platform. Why was this police officer so persistent?

'Take care now,' called Linda McLean, part of her feeling guilty for allowing Mel to travel. Best not to make a fuss, she rationalised. She couldn't prove anything.

So many kids were into drugs these days, but you might expect more from our better schools!

Mel struggled through the early afternoon crowds to the top end of the station. Ah, there it was, Platform 12. And the train for Stewarton was already waiting. Her mind was in a whirl. All she wanted was to get away from this girl Jane and her awful life. And why had that police officer stopped her? Did she think Mel had done something wrong? Was she following her now, even?

In fact, Officer McLean had not moved from the spot where they had spoken, but she was watching Mel's progress with interest. Suddenly she felt even more uneasy about this schoolgirl. 'Oh, no!' she whispered aloud, reaching for the radio clipped to her lapel. Instead of entering the barrier to the platform, Mel had veered off to the right and was heading down the stairs that led out into Argyle Street. She couldn't possibly have mistaken that for the platform. 'Maybe she's just changed her mind. You worry too much!' she said to herself, replacing her radio.

By now Mel had reached the bottom of the staircase and was slumped on a bench in the hallway that gave out into the street. All kinds of thoughts were racing through her fevered brain. She simply couldn't cope anymore. These 'episodes' at school were becoming more and more frequent and everyone was noticing. She'd broken down now in three classes, as well as in other places with her friends. She could no longer concentrate on her schoolwork – even though it meant everything to her. She wondered if she had been under some kind of unconscious stress, always striving to impress herself and others. And maybe it was all now coming to a sticky end. Or was it something more sinister? Was there something 'unnatural' going on in her life? How could she possibly go home when her school situation was breaking down in this way? Where *could* she go? Mel sat, alone and lonely, as the clouds of despair gathered round her, penetrating her very bones like the *haar*, the cold and desolate sea-mist that drifts over the North Sea to Scotland from Scandinavia.

Chapter 13

Jane guided her trolley carefully through the revolving door at Asda. It always annoyed her when people strayed from the middle and brought the door to a standstill. Outside she paused and surveyed her full trolley. It was a beautiful afternoon, but that meant nothing to her.

'Oh, hello there! I hardly recognised you, Jane. My, you're such a bonnie lass, your mum would be proud of you.' Jane managed a smile when she saw her friend, Ruby, approaching. 'But you're not too happy, are you, love? Smile or no smile, I can always tell.'

'There's no fooling you, is there, Ruby?' Jane tried to laugh, but broke down instead. 'Ruby, I feel terrible. But I don't want to bug you with it.'

Ruby put a comforting arm around her shoulder. 'Look, pet, I don't start my shift for another forty minutes. I was going to buy a few things myself, but that can wait. Come on and I'll treat you to a wee cup of coffee. You don't need to tell me about it if you don't want to, but one thing's certain – you're not going home in that state.'

'Thanks, Ruby.' Together they negotiated their way back through the revolving door and headed for the cafeteria, which was open-plan at the side of the main hallway. They chose a table for two next to the wall.

'Just park your trolley here where we can keep an eye on it,' said Ruby. 'My, you've been busy today, haven't you? You sit here, Jane, and I'll get us fixed up.'

When Ruby returned a few minutes later with the coffees, Jane was unsure about how much to tell her. But twenty minutes later, Ruby knew all about Jane walking out on her father and brother, her short stay in the Hector Campbell Centre, and how she had felt compelled to come back home. Ruby was horrified to hear that she had been exposed to such dangers. 'It's a scandal, Jane,' she fumed. 'To think the Council can do nothing better for a vulnerable wee lassie than to put you up in a glorified doss-house with all the riff-raff of the day! Is that what I've been paying my taxes for all these years? It's a damned disgrace, so it is!'

The two sat in silence for a moment, then Ruby's voice mellowed. 'I know just what ye' mean about your dad,

Jane. The likes of you and me, we just keep going back for more, don't we? I wish I knew the answer to that one!'

'I can't just leave him to die, can I, Ruby?'

'Of course not, pet, of course not. But you're not responsible for his life either, are you? My advice is that you get back to that Social Work Department right now and tell them everything. Tell them what it was like in that Centre. Tell them you can't leave your dad, but you're getting next to no housekeeping money and you can't make ends meet. And, Jane, whatever else is bothering you – just tell them that, too. Eh?'

Ruby's comments opened the floodgates. Jane's entire body stiffened as she exerted all her energy into an effort of self-control. But she was fighting a losing battle. At first it was a soft whimper. Ruby was enjoying a long sip of her coffee and had to bend her 'good' ear in Jane's direction before she could be sure the noise was coming from her. Ruby replaced her cup rapidly and her eyes widened. Jane's upper lip was quivering, then it was her entire mouth. Next her head began to shake convulsively, then her arms, her hands, and her entire body – and at each stage the soft whimper notched up gradually into a loud wail. Jane's legs shuddered against the underside of the table, and as the energy transferred itself her cup and saucer began a crazy dance until they launched themselves like lemmings over the edge. There was a harsh clatter as they hit the floor. Already every eye in the cafeteria had turned to witness Jane's breakdown.

'Oh, my poor wee soul,' muttered Ruby, reaching over and enveloping Jane in her ample bosom, where the convulsive sobbing continued loud and unabated for several minutes.

The Duty Manager appeared as if by magic. She remained a discreet distance from Ruby's table, but signalled to one of the assistants, who set about clearing away the crockery and mopping up the spillage.

Eventually, as if a storm had passed, the force of Jane's wailing was spent and she settled into a relative calmness, broken only occasionally by loud, wracking sobs. Neither she nor Ruby moved an inch.

The Manager picked her moment and moved closer. 'Hello, Ruby,' she said gently. 'Is this your daughter?'

'Unfortunately, no,' replied Ruby. 'If only she were!' There was a pause. 'She's a friend, but she's got some . . . eh . . . domestic trouble right now. Look, Margaret, I'm due on duty myself soon, but I can't leave her like this . . .' As her voice trailed off, Ruby looked imploringly at her boss, who understood instantly.

'Of course not. I'll change your shift, Ruby. You see that she gets home OK. Do you want me to call a taxi?'

'That would be grand, Margaret, thanks a million.'

Five minutes later, still clinging to Ruby, Jane was led out to the taxi and her shopping was loaded into the boot. Once they were on their way, Ruby spoke. 'You need taking care of tonight, my lass. And by the sound of things there's nobody at home capable of that. We'll drop your shopping off at Morton Street, then you'll come home with me. My man's on the night-shift, so we'll have the place to ourselves. What do you say?'

'Thanks, Ruby.' Jane's voice was hardly more than a whisper.

'You can speak to me some more if you wish, but you'll get a good night's sleep anyway. And tomorrow if you're up to it, we'll go down and see the social worker together.'

'You're a gem, Ruby!' she said, managing a weak smile.

The two looked at each other, then Ruby started to laugh, which made Jane laugh, and the laughter grew until they were almost hysterical. Ruby could see the anxious eyes of the taxi-driver squinting at them through his rear-view mirror. 'Don't you worry about us, son,' she called. 'Just you keep driving!' Ruby turned to Jane again. 'Aye, if only I could live up to my name more often!'

Jane peered anxiously out of the bus window. She and Ruby had talked long into the night, and Jane managed a few hours of restless, fitful sleep. In a way she wished they were going to the Social Work office that she'd been to last Saturday morning, but she realised that was only for emergencies outside normal hours. Today she would have to go to her local office and deal with strangers all over again.

There had been no sign of her dad and Barry when she and Ruby had delivered the groceries yesterday, but at least they hadn't been lying on the floor in a heap.

'Here we are. Next stop,' said Ruby, already rising from the seat they shared. Jane's tummy was doing cartwheels as she saw the former school building that had the words 'Social Work Department' on a large sign outside it.

They had to wait in a rather dingy waiting room for about fifteen minutes. In the corner was a play area with soft toys, and Jane was absorbed by the antics of two young children playing there. She was grateful for something to take her mind off her ordeal for a while.

The receptionist interrupted. 'The Duty Officer will see you now, Jane. Would you like to come through?'

Jane tried to swallow, but realised her throat was very dry. She was also aware that she was breaking out in a nervous sweat, and hoped against hope that her deodorant would hold up! 'Can my friend come with me?' she asked.

'Of course, if you want her to.'

'Are you sure, Jane?' asked Ruby.

'Yes. Please,' said Jane firmly.

They were shown into a small interview room and were greeted by a friendly gentleman. 'Hello there. I'm Brian Jackson, the Duty Officer today. It's Jane, isn't it?'

97

'Yes.' Jane hoped her voice didn't really sound as croaky as it did to her. 'And this is my friend, Ruby, who looked after me last night.'

'Good. Sit down, and let's get a few details first of all. Would you like a drink of water? Just help yourself.'

'Thanks,' said Jane, gratefully pouring a beaker from the cooled water container next to the wall. I am croaking, she thought to herself.

'Now then, give me your full name and address.'

Chapter 14

Molly was in a flap. She scurried along the corridor to the head teacher's office, knocked on the door loudly, and went in without waiting to be invited. Conveniently, Mr Hamilton was just finishing a telephone call and as he replaced the receiver he looked up in surprise at the agitated and slightly glowing figure in front of him. 'Molly! What's up?'

'Sorry to barge in, Mr Hamilton. But something dreadful's happened. And it's all my fault!'

'Sit down, Molly. Now, take your time.'

'It's the tuck shop money. It's disappeared.' She paused dramatically, awaiting some response.

Mr Hamilton obliged. 'Disappeared?'

'Yes. Someone's taken it. It's all gone.'

'Start at the beginning, Molly.'

'Well, as you know, we keep the day's takings in the office safe until there's enough for one of the admin girls to take it to the bank – every three days or so.' She sniffed and rummaged in her sleeve for a tissue. Mr Hamilton shifted in his chair, barely concealing his impatience. 'Yesterday was quite a slack day at the tuck shop and I . . . well, I was a bit pushed for time . . .'

'Yes, go on.'

'Well, I never handed the money in to the office.' Molly broke down. 'So you see, it's all my fault.'

'Did you lose the money?'

'No, no. And I hope you don't think I *took* it for anything!' she cried, defensively.

'Not at all, Molly. Now, carry on.'

'I left the girls to add up yesterday's and today's cash, and to hand it in to Christine.'

'Which girls?'

'The Fourth Year prefects. It was Victoria and Mel today. But according to Christine no money was handed in. And I hear Mel's gone home sick. I think she must have left the money unattended and forgot to hand it in – because she was feeling unwell.'

'Wait a minute. You left the *pupils* in charge of the money? How much?'

'There would have been about three hundred pounds
– at least.' Molly was aware of the Head's accusing look.
'They're good girls, those two. You know them yourself.
You could trust them with your life.'

'Have you spoken with them yet?'

'Victoria says she knows nothing about it. She was
locking up the cupboard and she assumed Mel was
handing in the money.'

'Mm . . .' Mr Hamilton paused thoughtfully. 'Melissa
. . . She lives down in Stewarton, doesn't she? It could
be that she was ill and has inadvertently taken the
money with her. I'll get Christine to give her a ring at
home. And I'll have another word with Victoria myself.
I'm sure there'll be some simple explanation. But I
think you should revise your procedures for handling
this money, Molly. The kids shouldn't be responsible for
the tuck shop. They have enough to think about with
their schoolwork.' He couldn't keep the rising anger out
of his voice. 'Situations like this just should not arise!'

'Yes, Mr Hamilton.' Molly slunk towards the door
like a schoolgirl who had just been ticked off. Before
leaving, she turned and asked hesitantly: 'You'll not be
phoning the police or anything, will you?'

'No, Molly. That would be a last resort. It's always
best to deal with these things in-house.' Molly knew he
was thinking about the school's reputation. 'I'm sure it

101

will turn up with Mel, but if not we'll have to have a full investigation.'

Five minutes later the phone on Mr Hamilton's desk buzzed. It was Christine, the school secretary. 'I'm sorry, Mr Hamilton. There's no reply at Melissa's. We've only got a mobile number and it appears to be switched off. They haven't given us an emergency contact either.'

'Thanks, Christine, but keep trying, will you?' He replaced the receiver and reached for his *Things to Do* pad. In his hurried scrawl he wrote: *Note to Year Group Heads: Get all students' home and emergency contacts up to date – pronto!*

Victoria was seething. For the first time in her life she'd had the humiliation of being called into the head teacher's office. Not that she'd been accused of anything, mind you, but there was a very large question mark over the missing tuck shop money. 'Obviously no one's going to suspect Mel,' she said to the large group that had gathered round, craving even the tiniest snippet of gossip. 'So I must be Suspect Number One. And I've never stolen a thing in my life!' The bell for the end of the day's classes had rung and they were making their way towards the main gates. 'The Head says he thinks Mel may have taken it with her by mistake, but he's not that daft. He's only playing for time.'

102

'What do you mean? Why couldn't Mel have taken it by mistake?' asked Saima, one of the crowd.

'Think about it,' said Victoria. She pulled up abruptly with one of her dramatic gestures. 'We're not talking about a few fivers or tenners you could slip into your purse and forget about. The tuck shop money comes in coins. There's all kinds. Mel and I had to sort them out and put them in plastic bags for the bank. They're bulky and they're heavy. Whoever took them knew exactly what they were doing. Mel couldn't have taken it by mistake. She must have forgotten and left the money lying around for anyone to pick up. I know she wasn't well, but she's landed us both in trouble.' Although she was genuinely upset about her friend, there was a part of Victoria that loved an audience, and she was indulging it to the full.

Julie in the meantime had been trying to contact Mel by phone. 'It's no good,' she said. 'Her mobile's still switched off – and I've had no reply to my texts.'

'Oh no, I hope she's not been kidnapped!' said Lisa, the Prophet of Doom.

'How could she have been kidnapped?' asked Nick, making it clear he didn't suffer fools gladly.

'Well, maybe someone in the school saw her with the money – a worker or someone – and forced her to go away with him.' Lisa was keen to prove she wasn't daft at all.

'Or maybe she had to leave the money because she was sick – and when she came back it had gone,' suggested Saima. 'Maybe she couldn't face it and she's run away.'

'*Mama mia*, she *has* been acting very strange recently . . .' said Angelo.

'. . . and I know for certain she's been getting things out of proportion,' added Nick.

It was Lisa who voiced what they'd all been fearing. 'You don't think she'll . . . go and do anything *silly*, do you?'

'I don't think she'll kill herself, if that's what you mean,' said Nick, but deep down fear was tying him in knots too.

There was an ominous silence.

Eventually it was broken by Raj. 'OK, why don't we go out to her house? Even if she's not well, she'd want this cleared up just as much as we do.'

'Good idea,' said Julie, 'but we can't *all* go.'

'You're right. So it should be you and Victoria,' suggested Raj.

'Suits me,' said Victoria. 'Does anyone know the way?'

'I don't even know her address,' said Julie. 'Do you?'

'Wha-at?' asked Nick. 'She's your best pal, for Heaven's sake!'

'Yeah, but she lives miles away in Stewarton. And she's got so much on at the weekends. We've never had a chance to visit her. We've always had to make do with our phones and e-mails.

Nick looked deflated. 'Fair enough.' Just as quickly, he brightened. 'I know! We can ask at the office. They'll have her address. Let's go back.' He turned and the whole crowd began to follow.

'Just a minute, folks. They won't let us all into the office,' said Victoria, causing everyone to halt for a second time. 'You lot go home. We'll let you know what happens in the morning.' The crowd began to drift away. Everyone realised that the story had been milked as far as it could for one day.

Nick was exasperated. '*Why* can't you give us her address? We're her friends!' The woman behind the window was being decidedly un-cooperative. 'If she's not well we've got a right to get in touch with her.'

'There's such a thing as confidentiality, young man. We can't just give out people's private details to anyone who asks!'

'But what if she's off for a while?' asked Julie. 'Won't the school want to know about it?'

'Of course. But there are procedures. Her Guidance Teacher can write or telephone. The Attendance Officer can visit. You just leave these things to us. Thank you very much.'

'Come on,' said Victoria. 'She's right. They have to have rules. I wouldn't want them to give out *my* information to anyone who asks. We'll just keep trying her phone.' They made their way back towards the gates.

Victoria stopped in her tracks, a look of terror on her face. 'Of course,' she said to the others eventually, 'something like this was bound to happen. You won't like this, Nick, but I've got to say it anyway. It may be that even though Mel doesn't *want* to take her own life, she feels she has no choice. The spirit that's been trying to get her might already be making its final move. Mel might do whatever it takes to avoid being possessed.'

'Victoria, this is no time for sick jokes,' shouted Nick.

'It's no joke!' Victoria retaliated. 'If this has happened, there's nothing you or I can do about it.' There was a stunned silence. 'Unless . . .' Victoria was obviously lost in thought.

'Unless what?' asked Raj.

'Unless there's someone at the Psychic Centre who can help us. There's things you can do to ward off evil spirits. I'm going to go straight there now. Mel is out there somewhere on her own. She needs our help. Can anyone come up with a better idea?'

'I think I prefer the kind of prayers I've been brought up with,' said Julie. 'I don't think I could go to that place with you, Victoria.'

'I'll see if my mum can suggest anything,' said Nick.

'That's OK. We can all do our own thing. But let's get busy. There's no telling what she could be going through right now,' said Victoria. And with that, Victoria strode off downhill, past Athole Gardens.

Chapter 15

As soon as the bell for the mid-morning break sounded the next day, Nick and Angelo raced from the Modern Languages department to the patio area at the back of the school. Julie had already grabbed a table. This morning there were no thoughts of lining up at the tuck shop, everyone had the same question on their minds: any news of Mel?

They were soon joined by Victoria, Raj and some of the onlookers from the previous afternoon. 'Ambulance chasers!' Victoria had called them. 'They're only interested in a bit of bad news. I hope they'll be thoroughly disappointed!'

'No joy,' said Julie. 'She wasn't in Geography.' There

was a collective groan. Everyone knew Mel hadn't turned up for Registration at nine o'clock, but they'd hoped she was just late.

'Is there any news at all?' asked Lisa.

'No,' answered Victoria. 'We all kept in touch with each other last night.' She indicated Julie, Angelo, Raj, Nick and herself. 'But we're none the wiser.'

'Did you go to the Psychic Centre?' asked Saima.

Victoria wrinkled her nose. 'Huh! A fat lot of good they were! They said Mel would have to come in for a consultation herself before they could advise. It was just a cop out.'

'Well . . .' began Nick, with an 'I told you so!' look on his face.

Victoria glared at him. 'Don't you start, Nick!'

Sensing the tension between them, Julie was quick to intervene. 'Angelo and I were going to go down to Stewarton and ask around when we got there, but my Mum heard us on the phone and put her foot down.'

'What did she say?' asked Lisa.

'She said we were making a fuss about nothing. If Mel went home sick we should just leave her in peace. And the school would sort out the business of the money.'

'It's not really about the money, though, is it?' asked Nick. 'OK, three hundred pounds is quite a lot, but it's no big deal. Mel had a good excuse for not looking after it properly.'

'Three hundred pounds!' whistled Lisa.

'£312.40, to be exact,' said Victoria.

'We should be more concerned about her state of mind!' said Nick, bristling again.

'What did your mum say about that?' asked Saima.

'Oh, she just got annoyed because I didn't speak to her earlier about Mel. She said it was a bit like locking the stable door after the horse had bolted. She said she would do what she could today. But she was right, wasn't she? She can't help Mel if Mel's not here.'

'I stopped at Athole Gardens on my way up this morning,' said Raj. 'I tried to work out why her dizzy spells started happening there.'

'And what did you find?' asked Nick.

'Nothing! That's just it, nothing. I looked all around the place from every angle. There were just the railings and the hedge, with the grass and the trees inside. Across the road there's nothing but ordinary houses, and it's the same on the other side of the Gardens. The whole thing's a mystery.'

Everyone sat or stood around in a glum silence for a while. 'Well, I can't stand just doing nothing,' said Nick eventually. 'I'm going to have another go at the office.'

'They won't tell us anything,' said Victoria.

'They can tell us if there's been any contact.'

But Nick was wrong. The office staff insisted that no information about fellow students would be divulged at any time for any reason, and that was that.

The bell rang for the end of break and they were making their way back to their classes, when Victoria caught sight of the head teacher patrolling the corridor. 'One last chance!' she said to her friends.

She approached the Head. 'Excuse me, Mr Hamilton. I was wondering if you'd heard any more about the tuck shop money. Mel's still off sick, so we haven't had any news.'

'No, there's no news at all, Victoria, and there seems to be no way of contacting Melissa.' He put on a rather grim face. 'If I don't hear in the course of the morning, I'll have to take more steps to get to the bottom of this.'

Victoria rejoined her friends, who had overheard the conversation. 'How come there's no way of contacting Mel?' she whispered. 'You'd think *they* would have her parents' number. And what does he mean by "take more steps"?'

Chapter 16

'My *full* name? It's . . .'

There was silence. Brian Jackson looked up from his notepad, puzzled.

'It's . . .' The butterflies in Jane's stomach had given way to a feeling of slight nausea and it seemed as though her whole body was shaking.

Ruby reached over and squeezed her hand.

'Yes?' prompted the social worker. He noticed Jane struggling again. 'It's just a formality – for the records, that's all.'

It took her nearly every muscle in her body to steady her hand enough to take a sip of water. She swallowed hard, then looked straight into Brian Jackson's eyes.

'My full name is Melissa-Jane Nicol. I live at 12 Morton Street.'

Ruby sat back in her chair with a big smile that said 'Well done!' Clearly, she sensed a bridge had been crossed.

'I've gone mad, I know I have!' she suddenly blurted out. 'I don't know what's happening to me. I . . .'

'Let's just take it easy – and slowly,' said Brian

Jane made a concerted effort to breathe slowly and deeply, a skill she'd learned in Drama class, but her hands wouldn't stop trembling.

'Now then,' continued Brian. 'Tell me about your family first.'

'I live with my dad and my brother. My mum's dead. I'm known at home as Jane.'

'And you're still at school?'

'Yes, I'm at Hillside High School.' A look of surprise flashed across Brian's face, but was gone before Jane looked up. Tears welled up in Jane's eyes. 'That's the problem . . .'

'Don't you like it there?' asked Brian.

'I love it . . . It's . . .' Jane broke down. 'I can't go on at home any longer . . .'

'Home?' asked Brian. 'Didn't you just say it was *school?*'

'Well, yes . . . Yesterday, I . . .'

'Go on, love,' whispered Ruby.

Jane reached for a tissue and wiped the tears off her cheeks, then blew her nose. Crying had allowed her nerves to calm down slightly. She cleared her throat, and went on. 'Yesterday I . . . I walked out of school with money that . . . that wasn't mine. I'd like you to phone them, please. The head teacher's name is Mr Hamilton. Tell him I'm all right and I'll get the money back as soon as possible.'

'That's my girl,' said Ruby, gently squeezing Jane's hand again.

'Could you call them right away, please? Oh . . . and tell them it's Mel – I'm known at school as Mel.'

Brian smiled. 'OK, Jane – or should I call you Mel?'

'Yes, it's confusing, isn't it?' She relaxed a little. 'You can take your pick, but I prefer Mel.' She managed to return the smile.

'Right, Mel it is. And please call me Brian. I *will* phone the school, Mel, but before that, start from the beginning. Why do you feel you're going mad?'

Mel took a refreshing gulp of water, sat back in the vinyl-covered lounge chair and poured out her heart. She told the social worker all about the family history, how her remaining family were killing themselves with drugs, how she was expected to hold things together, and her hair-raising experience at the Hector Campbell

Centre. Brian listened intently, but he hunched forward in his chair, fascinated, when she told him about her school experience.

'I was *determined* that my life wouldn't turn out like Dad and Barry's. I knew I was capable of more, but I could see no way out.' She looked earnestly at her friend. 'I've never seen anyone escape from a life like that. Have you, Ruby?'

'It's hard, love, but it can be done.' Deep down, Ruby knew that what she really meant was: *I couldn't, but I hope you can.*

'All I could see round about me was death and decay,' Mel went on. 'I needed to come up with some way out. Some way, so that people wouldn't treat me like dirt. *"Oh, she's from Morton Street. Her dad's a junkie! Her brother's a crack-head!"* All I wanted was an equal chance. But . . . But I think I went about it the wrong way.'

'How *did* you go about it?' asked Brian.

Mel paused. She was still trembling, but the nausea was passing with the realisation that a major hurdle had been overcome. She *could* talk to this man, so she was determined to go on. 'I got in touch with my aunt, my dad's sister. She's well off and lives down in Stewarton. She doesn't want anything to do with us – at least I don't think so. She's never very friendly. But I persuaded her to get me enrolled in Hillside High School and to give them her address. I was at the local school before that, but there was talk of it closing down. None of my friends there wanted to learn. It was a waste of time. Dad never objected. I don't think he even cared! She wasn't keen, but she came round when she realised this could be a way out for me.'

'And wasn't it?'

'Sort of . . . I suppose it *could* have been. Everyone there was so nice. And they all seemed to come from decent backgrounds. I didn't want to stick out like a sore thumb and come up against all the old prejudices.' Tears welled up again at the memory. 'So I invented a . . . *a different life*.' Mel looked up guiltily, tears still in her eyes. Brian gave her an encouraging smile and she pressed on. 'I made out as if my aunt and uncle were my parents, who took me on foreign trips and sent me to horse riding and stuff – even though I haven't seen them since the day I enrolled!

'And it worked. I even changed my name. My dad always called me Jane because he didn't like the name my mum had insisted on. *Melissa-Jane*. He thought it was too pretentious. But "Mel" suited me at school. When I was with my friends, even I began to believe in my good fortune.

'I did really well. I picked things up quite easily. I

actually loved the schoolwork, especially Art and Music and Sports. It was all so different to what I had before. I knew I wouldn't get a chance to study in Morton Street – too cold in my room for a start – so I always went to the Homework Club. That way I didn't have to take much work home.'

Ruby looked at Mel sadly. 'So you were two different people: Mel, the well-off, bright kid at school, and Jane, overworked, tired and cracking up at home.'

'Things got so bad at home . . .' Mel reached for a tissue, unsure whether she should go on, or even whether she *could* go on.

Several minutes passed in silence. Suddenly, with a wracking sob, Mel blurted out, 'I must be losing my mind! I mean . . . I've even got a friend who thinks I'm possessed or something, but I know it's not that. I think I'm going mad.'

'What makes you say that?' asked Brian gently.

'At school I just seem to forget I'm anyone other than Mel from Stewarton. Then I'll be sitting at my desk or whatever and I suddenly just lose the place. I'm aware of the school, I'm aware of this body, but it's not *me*. Then I have flashbacks. I see Jane, with her life in Morton Street. I don't know who she is, it's like another life altogether . . . and it's only later – usually when I'm on my way home – that I realise I was seeing the other side of *my own life*. I don't know why this is happening . . . it's like I've lost control.

'Then yesterday for the first time my two lives seemed to clash together. I was counting up the money from the tuck shop, and I just sort of, well . . . *took* it. But I never thought about breaking the law, or anything . . . I was so confused – I remember even going to the Central Station as if I had a home to go to in Stewarton. It was only when I discovered I didn't have a ticket that I realised what I was doing. So I went to the Underground instead and headed for my real home. It wasn't until I got to Asda that I became aware I was lugging the money with me. And I'm afraid . . .' Mel bowed her head dejectedly. 'I'm afraid I went on a spree.'

'And that's when you met Ruby?' asked Brian.

'Yes, thank God I did! I don't know how I could have let myself get so far gone. It's not as if I didn't know the spells were happening more often . . . But I guess I didn't know who to turn to. Now I just need it all to stop. I'll return the money and work to pay off the rest. Mr Hamilton can phone the police if he wants – as long as the visions stop . . .'

Brian looked at his watch. 'The school will be wondering where you are. I think the first thing we should do is give them a call. You nip back into the waiting room and I'll have a chat with Mr Hamilton.'

Ten minutes later, Mel and Ruby were called back into the interview room. 'Well, I've had a word with Mr Hamilton,' Brian began, 'and he's delighted you're OK. But he is worried about you. You'll be pleased to hear he's not going to press charges, but it's on one condition. He wants you to promise that you'll accept counselling so this sort of thing will never happen again. Your future at the school is under review, but we'll cross that bridge when we reach it. I'll get a social worker assigned to your family and we'll try to help with that side. Mr Hamilton put me on to the school psychologist, a Mrs Conway. She told me you and her son, Nick, are friends, and that he's been very worried about you – she's on her way over right now – she'll be here in about twenty minutes.' He paused. 'I really think it would be a good idea for you to talk to her, Mel.'

'Yes. Yes, I will. It's really good of her to come over . . . but there's no question of me ever going back to school again.'

Chapter 17

'Come on, come on! Get a move on!' Nick's mum tended to avoid the Clyde Tunnel whenever she could. She seemed to have an unhappy knack of getting stuck in it! Today, however, using the tunnel was unavoidable – it was the only route she could take to the Social Work Department. The traffic was heavy and her Renault Clio was inching forward in the queue. She was worried that the girl might disappear again. Her son had drawn her attention to this girl and Mrs Conway didn't like what she'd heard. Now the girl was waiting for her in a Social Work office, and if she didn't get there soon, she could easily up and off once again – and this time she might do something silly!

Mrs Conway forced herself to breathe deeply, in spite of the acrid exhaust fumes in the tunnel that seemed to seek out every tiny opening, even with the windows closed, and force their way through. She must stay calm; otherwise she'd be a bundle of nerves once she arrived and no use to anyone.

It seemed to work. In five minutes she was through the jam, and then it was only a short drive to the Social Work Department.

Within seconds of entering the office, she was introduced to Brian, Mel and Ruby and was sitting with them in the interview room. To save Mel repeating herself, Brian filled Mrs Conway in with the essential details, pausing every so often for Mel to nod in agreement. At the end of the story he stood up. 'Right. Why don't I leave you alone together for a chat? If you need me I'll be in the main office just across the hall.'

'And I'll wait for you in the waiting room. You'll manage fine on your own now, pet,' said Ruby.

Once they were alone, Mel was the first to speak. 'Thanks very much for coming to see me, Mrs Conway. I'm sorry to put you to this bother.'

Mrs Conway smiled. 'It's no bother. Actually I was glad to get the call, because Nick told me about you and I've been hoping to speak to you. Now, can you tell me a bit more about these "dizzy spells" you've been experiencing?'

'They're quite scary. Do you really think you can help me? Sometimes I . . . I just don't know who I am. And I worry that I'm going crazy. The dizzy spells seem to be happening more and more . . . It's like I'm being taken over by a stranger. Then when they've passed, I remember it's the other side of my own life after all. It doesn't make much sense, does it?'

'It makes perfect sense, Mel. And let me tell you right away that it's highly unlikely you're going crazy – or that you have a serious mental illness, to put it professionally. What you're describing is a natural reaction to the stresses you've been under. These amnesia attacks – brief spells of losing your memory, if you like – are part of that. Think about it. There's enormous pressure on you at home. You have to do all the cooking and cleaning; then there's the shopping, when you can hardly make ends meet. The money supply is drying up while you watch your family go downhill, and somehow you've got to stave off depression yourself. It's no surprise that you want to pretend it's not really happening. What you've found out is that no matter how strongly you deny them, the facts won't be ignored.'

'I never thought of it like that.'

'And while you're *trying* to ignore them, there's a lot more pressure at school. You've had to cope with your studies, as well as keeping up appearances, sticking to all the scenarios you made up. So to cope with *that*, you started to think of these scenarios as real. The brain is a mysterious and powerful thing and it can play tricks on you. Quite frankly, I'm amazed you didn't have a major breakdown ages ago, Mel. It's very much to your credit that you've held your life together. So it's no wonder that your mind complains about all this by playing a few tricks now and then, is it?'

'Not when you put it like that!'

'This is all to do with what we call your *identity*, Mel. Unfortunately this kind of thing is becoming more and more common.'

Mel lifted her gaze. 'You mean there are other people like this?'

'That's right. You're by no means the only one. But I have to tell you, Mel, the danger is that if the situation goes unchecked, if you refuse to integrate – or bring together the different areas of your life – then it *can* lead to serious mental health problems.'

'But how can I start to do that?' Mel sounded desperate. 'If I admit to what I've been doing, will it start to get better?'

'That's certainly part of the solution. You need to stop *meaning* to be two different people.'

'But then I'm stuck back where I began. Life at home

certainly won't change. And my dad feels he's got nothing to live for. And . . .' Mel's brow furrowed. 'I can't just pick up where I left off with my friends!'

'Well, why don't we start with what we can do just now? Let's begin with your name. It would probably be better if you decided on *one* name and stuck to that. Don't you agree?'

'Yes. My dad likes to call me Jane, but I know I'll always think of myself as Mel. My mum liked the name Melissa, so in a sense it keeps me in touch with her.'

'Right. Step One: always call yourself Mel, short for Melissa. You can *answer* to Jane if your dad insists on calling you that, but you must always think of yourself as Mel. Agreed?'

'Yes, but it won't be easy admitting to everyone that I'm Mel from Morton Street!'

'True, but do you really have a choice? It's not going to be easy, but you'll have to take things one step at a time. We need to get you back to school and take it from there.'

Mel was thoughtful for a moment. Could she ever face her friends again? Could she cope with the humiliation? And what about their anger – could she cope with the inevitable rejection? 'I just don't think that's an option, Mrs Conway. I've treated my friends like dirt, lying to them non-stop. I think they'd be better off without me. Anyway, I've spent almost a hundred pounds of the school's money, which I'll have to pay back. Ruby can get me a job in Asda. I've never had time before, but that's all changed now that I'm leaving school. Could you take the rest of the money back for me?' Mel pointed to her school bag. 'It's rather heavy, I'm afraid.'

'I'll see to that all right. But you have to seriously think about your future, Mel. The way ahead for you is education. You can't just give that up.'

'Oh, I won't. I'll get a job, but I'll go to college as well.'

'I'm not convinced that's the way forward.'

'But surely it's for the best under the circumstances, Mrs Conway? I've not been a good influence at school, have I? Mr Hamilton probably won't let me back anyway.'

'I suppose we can't pre-empt the head teacher's decision, but I'd like to have a word with him.'

'I'd rather you had a word with Nick, Mrs Conway. Would you ask him to explain everything to my friends? There's one in particular, Victoria – she's convinced there are spirits at work.' Mel smiled ruefully. 'She'll be driving herself mad with worry!'

'I'll talk to Nick. But think about what you've just said, Mel. They're your *friends*. It won't be good for you to just cut them out of your life because you think you can't face them. They can help you come to terms with everything. Think seriously about that, will you, Mel?'

'I will.' But there was a faraway look in Mel's eye, and the answer was just too glib, too pat. Mrs Conway knew Mel wasn't convinced.

Chapter 18

When Brian Jackson and Ruby returned to the interview room they were pleased to hear that Mel and Mrs Conway had been making some progress, at least. 'The immediate challenge for us now, Mel, is where you're going to live,' said Brian.

'I'd love to take you in with me, pet,' said Ruby, 'but . . . Well, things aren't always just right in my house either.' Unconsciously, she rubbed her right jaw, and her eyes moistened. 'It wouldn't be good for you.'

Mel leaned over and placed her hand firmly on the back of Ruby's other hand. Nothing more needed to be said.

'You can always go back to the Hector Campbell

Centre, but I don't think that appeals to you, does it?' asked Brian

'No. I would only go there as a last resort. And even then . . .' Mel shuddered.

'What about continuing to stay at home?' asked Brian.

Mel didn't answer. She felt torn between loyalty to her family and the need to break free from them.

'I don't think that would be in your best interests,' said Mrs Conway. 'We've got to make sure at all costs that you don't sink further into depression. We could look at the possibility of fostering. It's very hit-and-miss, I'm afraid. It all depends on who's available and whether there's a waiting list, but how does that appeal, Mel?'

'I'd certainly consider it.'

'You could set up in a flat by yourself, under our supervision. That's quite common, but a lot of young people tend to get lonely living on their own,' said Brian.

'I don't think it would be any worse than the situation I'm in right now.'

'You've just given me an idea,' said Mrs Conway. 'Now, why didn't I think of that before?' All three looked at her expectantly. 'I'd like to make a phone call first. Can I use an office, Brian?'

'Sure, follow me.' He led the way and Mel was left alone with Ruby.

A wave of remorse swept over Mel. 'What have I done, Ruby? I don't think I can go through with this.'

'Don't worry, Mel. That's the worst over now, you'll see. The only way is up!' Ruby grinned, and they both started to laugh hysterically.

'Oh, don't, Ruby!' Mel pleaded. 'Don't start again! I nearly died laughing in the taxi.'

Soon Mrs Conway returned with Brian and she was smiling. 'I think we've come up with something that might just interest you, Mel. Let's see what you think.'

Mrs Conway and Brian took their seats again. Mel's eyes widened as the plan was put to her.

'Right. You two go on ahead and I'll get the bus home,' suggested Ruby.

'No, no. I'll run you home first, Ruby,' said Mrs Conway.

'I'll follow on later,' said Brian. 'That'll give you a chance to look things over.'

'And I'll let you know as soon as possible what's happening, Ruby,' said Mel. She held Ruby's hand again. Mel's heart was bursting with gratitude, but physically she felt drained. 'And thanks, Ruby. I think you've probably saved my life!'

'Then you make the most of it,' said Ruby. She smiled fondly at Mel and kissed her on the cheek.

'OK,' said Mrs Conway, 'let's head off.'

The car pulled up outside a white semi-detached two-storey house with a neat front garden. Yet again, Mel was going into unknown territory, and already she was missing Ruby's comforting presence. She closed the car door and looked at the house. She couldn't have hoped for a nicer place, but her nerves were playing up again. She felt reluctant to impose herself on a total stranger. And it was embarrassing, having to meet yet another 'middle class' person, who would inevitably know about her background. Brian and Mrs Conway had been helpful, but it hadn't been easy talking about everything. It's my only hope, she assured herself. And it'll just be temporary.

Steeling herself, she followed Mrs Conway through the garden gate.

She was about to stop Mrs Conway from going any further when the front door opened. 'Come in! Come in! You're very welcome, Mel. My, it'll be nice to have some young company about the house!' said the sprightly, silver-haired elderly lady who stood in the doorway.

'Now, Mum,' said Mrs Conway, 'let's not get ahead of

ourselves. This visit is just to see if this arrangement would suit *both of you*, remember? Mel, meet my mother, Mrs Prentice.'

'Very nice to meet you, Mrs Prentice,' said Mel, feeling awkward.

'Och, call me Irene. If we're going to be living under the same roof, I want us to be friends.' With that she gave Mel a friendly squeeze and led her inside.

Mel was immediately impressed by how bright, clean and modern the house was. It was not at all how she imagined an older person's house to be. In the living room was a white, leather three-piece suite with patterned cushions that matched the light blue carpet and curtains. There was a mahogany fireplace with a living-flame gas fire, and to the right of that was a magnificent wide-screen TV set in a cabinet with a hi-fi and a VCR. Mel didn't like to stare, but she was sure there was a silver-coloured DVD player there as well.

'Sit down, Mel. We'll have a wee cuppa first before I show you round. And once you're settling in I'll get the dinner on,' said Irene.

'I really don't want to impose, Mrs . . . I mean, Irene,' said Mel.

'Oh, there's no question of that!' said Irene. 'I'm fed up rattling around in this house by myself. It's too big for just one person, you know. I've been wanting to take in someone for quite some time.'

Irene smiled and went off to the kitchen. Mel and Nick's mum relaxed on the couch as they listened to the comforting, domestic sound of clinking china. Mel was beginning to feel she had landed on her feet, but there was still one thing bothering her . . .

'Did you say anything about the money I took?' she asked.

'Yes, Mel,' said Mrs Conway firmly. 'But my mother trusts my judgement. I know all about your excellent reputation at school. You were under stress yesterday. I know you're not a thief. And I hope we'll be working together – regardless of whether you go back to school or not. We can make sure that type of stress never comes back. So it's a pretty small risk Irene and I are taking, isn't it?'

'Thanks,' said Mel and the relief showed on her face.

In no time at all, Irene came in with tea and hot, buttered scones. 'I don't want you to feel under any obligation, Mel,' she said as she poured the tea, 'but you *are* very welcome to live here if that suits you. The children moved out years ago and things have not been the same since Henry died. I've turned the upstairs sitting room into a bedroom, so I tend to live on this floor. It saves my old legs on the stairs! There's plenty of room upstairs now.'

'Thanks very much, Irene. Staying here would be like a dream come true, but I don't know if my dad and brother could manage without me. I'll have to think about it for a bit.'

'I know, my dear. You can have a look around anyway and we'll see what happens.'

Mel's heart was bursting. A staircase with a deep pile carpet; a bedroom with central heating *and* a TV; and her own bathroom on the top floor. It seemed too good to be true.

There was a knock on the front door and when Mrs Prentice answered it, Mel heard Brian Jackson introduce himself.

'Since Mel has now asked for our support, we'll need to check out any arrangements. I hope you don't mind; it's just a formality.' Mel made her way back downstairs.

'Not at all,' replied Mrs Prentice. 'Unless I'm mistaken, Mel seems pleased – just as I am. It's just that she's worried about her family, isn't that right, dear?'

'Yes. I just don't know if I could abandon them. It would be great for me here, but I would be worried sick the whole time.'

'It wouldn't be a case of you abandoning them,' said Brian. 'We can offer assistance – like a Home Help service, for example. And you'd be able to visit as often as you liked. But you can't be expected to run their lives for them, Mel.'

'No, I suppose not.' She turned to Mrs Conway. 'I'll need to get that job, though – to pay for my keep here, as well as to pay back the school . . .'

'Oh, don't worry about giving me anything, dear,' Irene interjected. 'The mortgage was paid off when Henry died and he left me well provided for. One more mouth to feed won't make the slightest difference. In any case, you'd be doing *me* a favour. It'll be nice looking after someone again!'

'And don't forget, Mel, you'd be entitled to a rent allowance, and if you stayed on at school the Child Benefit you already get would continue, *plus* now that you're sixteen you'd get a bursary from the Education Department,' added Brian.

'Thanks. I would like to make *some* contribution, Irene,' said Mel, then turned to face Brian. 'But even if I wanted to, I don't know if I'd be allowed back to school. Don't forget – I gave a false address and made up new parents. I was there under false pretenses.'

'Well, we can work that out in due course.'

So what do you think? Do you want to give it a try?' Irene said, then saw Mel's hesitation. 'Why don't you have another look upstairs?'

'Thanks, I'd like that.'

As she climbed the stairs, her feet sinking once more into the thick carpet, Mel wondered why these people were being so nice to her. Surely she didn't deserve such treatment? She'd lied, she'd stolen, she came from a family of drug addicts . . . She entered the bedroom and could hardly believe the relative luxury that surrounded her. Her mind went back to the house in Morton Street. She sat on the bed for a moment, overcome with a feeling of guilt.

And then it struck her. This was not only her one chance to break free from the life she despised, it was also the only way she could help her family. She would go mad living at home, and what use would that be to anybody? There would be no university, no future. She knew her problems were by no means over, but at least she'd been thrown a lifeline here – and a very comfortable one at that.

She made her way back down to the living room. The three adults looked at her expectantly.

'I'd like to take you up on your offer, Irene.'

Chapter 19

At 8:35 the next morning Mrs Conway pulled into her usual parking spot at the side of the school. Nick had long since stopped coming in with her, preferring to meet up with his friends instead. She made her way to the head teacher's office, knocked and entered. 'Well, here it is.' She placed a bulky bag on to Mr Hamilton's desk. 'The vanishing tuck shop money and Mel's receipt from the supermarket.'

'Well done! And what about Mel? Has she come in with you?'

Mrs Conway sighed. 'I'm afraid not. She's taken an emotional battering, and she feels she can't come back. But I'd like to work on her. Have you made any decision about her yet? I was hoping we could keep her on the school roll in the meantime and put her absence down as "Illness".'

'That's what I'd like to do, but I'll have to get in touch with the Divisional Office first – the decision's not entirely down to me. I'm as keen as you are to get her through this crisis. I've written to her aunt and asked her to come in for a chat. We'll see what happens there first, then I'll discuss it with the Office. I've always admired Melissa – she's an outstanding student – so I'll see what I can do. Just keep me informed, will you?'

'Certainly. Mel asked me to explain everything to Nick and he's taken it upon himself to tell their friends. Mel wanted that anyway. I'm sure we can rely on him to be discreet. Their reaction will be crucial, I feel. Fingers crossed!'

At the start of Maths class, Mr Guppy was checking the names on his list. 'Jonathan . . . Victoria . . . Kenny . . . Aisha . . . Melissa . . .' He looked up when there was no answer. 'Melissa?'

'Absent, Sir,' Nick explained. 'She went home sick yesterday and she may be off for a while.'

Victoria glared at him. She didn't like someone else having information about *her* best friend before she did.

Nick read the situation and leaned towards Victoria. 'I'll fill you in at break,' he whispered. 'We'll go round to the patio and grab a table for the five of us.'

The break couldn't come quickly enough. As soon as the class was dismissed, Victoria managed to get word to Julie, Raj and Angelo, and then pelted out to secure a picnic table before they were all taken. She wisely chose one that was in a shaded area, slightly away from the rest.

Once they had all gathered, Nick cleared his throat. 'Mel had some kind of a breakdown yesterday and my mum was called out to see her last night.' He paused. 'Mel took the tuck shop money.'

'What?!' There were gasps all round.

'But she's returned it, so wait till I've told you the whole story. It appears she comes from a very hard background. There's all kinds of problems – all she wanted was to be accepted and given a chance here, so she made up those stories about her parents being well-off.'

Julie stopped with her spoon midway between her tub of yogurt and her lips. 'You mean she *doesn't* do horse riding and skiing and all that?'

'Correct. She invented all that to give herself a better chance here.'

'She was telling me about her drama club and how she could be getting a leading part . . .'

'Try to understand, Julie. Things were getting really bad at home and she was under pressure to keep up appearances here.'

'But that doesn't explain her visions, does it? There's more to it than that, Nick,' said Victoria.

'Which is why I asked you to wait till you've heard the whole story!' Nick had finally lost his patience with Victoria. 'And all that guff you've been spouting about *Doppelgängers* or whatever, has only been making matters worse. If you must know, she's been having *amnesia* attacks. She was getting so confused with her double life that her memory was switching off, and while it was off she was getting flashbacks of her home life, which just made her even *more* confused. Then when she remembered it all, she couldn't confide in any of us, because that would be giving the game away, wouldn't it? And you had her marked down as being *possessed* or something.'

Victoria sat there, speechless, her bottom lip quivering slightly. She had never felt more humiliated. There was an awkward silence and everyone was looking away, nobody knowing what to say.

Eventually she got up. 'Well, I can see you think it's all my fault.'

Nick knew he'd gone too far. 'No, Victoria, honestly we don't. I'm only saying . . .'

'Leave it, Nick. It's obvious my opinions are not welcome. I'll go before I cause any more damage.' Victoria made a great scene of gathering her things and storming off.

Nick started to follow her, but was stopped by Julie. 'Leave her. She'll come round. She just needs some time by herself to calm down. Mel was her best friend . . . You could have been a bit more sensitive, Nick.'

'I know. But she really bugged me with all that stuff. Anyway, our main concern is Mel. She was desperate, so she took the money to feed her family. She returned it when she came to her senses, but now she feels like she can't face any of us. She thinks she's let us all down and we'll never want to see her again. So . . . ?'

The other two boys had remained silent until now, but Raj finally spoke. 'I think it's a really sad story. She hasn't let *me* down; she's the one who's been suffering. And nothing's ever too much trouble when you ask *her* for help. We've got to support her.'

'I agree,' said Julie. 'Sorry about my reaction. I was only thinking of myself. I'm totally gobsmacked, but she's one of the best people I've ever known.'

'We've got to try to see her,' Angelo chipped in. 'Let her know we're still her friends. If she won't come to school, maybe we could meet her somewhere else. Get her to come to the café, she likes a good *cappuccino*.'

'Yeah, but *how* do we persuade her to come?' asked Raj. 'Where is she now, Nick?'

Nick explained about her staying with his grandmother.

'Cosy for you!' Raj was about to give Nick the customary thump on the arm when he noticed everyone glaring at him. Realising his joke was in bad taste, he hastily withdrew. 'Sorry,' he mumbled.

'She's staying there until further notice,' Nick continued. 'It was her birthday recently, and now that she's sixteen she can get a flat of her own. She'll be all right with my gran just now – everybody gets on with her.'

'I know what we can do,' said Julie. 'If the mountain won't come to Mohammed, Mohammed must go to the mountain.'

'That's the kind of thing Victoria would say! What does it mean?' asked Nick.

'It means I have an idea.'

They all listened intently as Julie outlined her plan.

'But what about Victoria?' asked Angelo.

'That's up to her. We should all treat her a bit more *delicately*, but if I know her, she'll want to be involved too.'

'Great,' said Nick. 'I'll speak to my gran and we'll get the arrangements made.'

Chapter 20

It was another bright Saturday morning. Mel let out a sigh as she pushed back her soft duvet. Lying in her new bed, she couldn't help comparing her surroundings to what she had left in Morton Street. The wall was painted in a calming lilac shade, with a white mosaic stencil pattern forming a border along the top of the walls. There were vertical blinds and curtains with floral tiebacks on the window. She had her own dressing table and on a corner unit stood a fourteen-inch TV and a small hi-fi with separate speakers. Her feet sunk into the soft, fleecy rug as she got out of bed.

Irene's voice drifted up from downstairs. 'Is that you up and about, Mel? Breakfast's ready whenever you are.'

'Thanks, Irene, I'll be right down.'

In the kitchen, the table was set. Irene always let her make her own choice for breakfast. This morning it was fresh fruit juice, a bowl of cereal with added fruit, followed by tea and toast.

I'm in the lap of luxury, Mel thought to herself. Yet her heart was still heavy and she had a nervous feeling in the pit of her stomach. Her mind couldn't help returning to the thought of her dad and Barry in Morton Street.

'Have you heard how things are at home?' asked Irene, as if reading Mel's mind.

'Yes. Brian Jackson told me that Dad has agreed to have the Home Help service, and they'll call in regularly to help him get organised. But I don't know if it'll make much difference with his drug habit.'

Mel thought back to her conversation with Brian. Her dad had said he wasn't really surprised that she'd left, and he wanted her to do well.

'Brian wanted me to have a break for a while, then he's going to take me back next week to have a talk with Dad.'

'Well, just you rest up in the meantime, dear.'

'Thanks. Oh, and Nick's mum is coming over to see me this afternoon. I don't know if she mentioned?'

'Yes, she did. I'm going down to the bowling club, so you can have a nice wee chat by yourselves.'

At half past two Mel was watching a re-run of *Hollyoaks*. Half her attention was on the storyline, while the other half was marvelling about how much a life can change in a matter of days. But while her life had changed for the better, she knew her future was by no means certain. She felt completely daunted by the idea of having to start all over again, leaving good friends and a good school behind, and trying to find a way forward elsewhere.

Her thoughts were interrupted by the sound of a key in the front door. Then Nick's mum called out: 'Hello, Mel! Are you there?'

'Yes, I'm in here! I'm on my own. Mrs Prentice has gone to her bowling.'

'Good!' Mrs Conway came in and quickly made herself at home. 'I hope I'm not interrupting your programme.'

'No, no. I was just passing the time, waiting for you. Shall I make a cup of tea?'

'No thanks, not just yet. I thought we'd get right down to business, if that's OK with you?'

'That's fine.'

Mrs Conway settled herself on the settee. 'So . . . How are you, Mel? Do you think it's working out for you here?'

'Well, from my side, definitely. I've never had it so

good! Your mum is like the grandmother I never had. I don't know how *she* feels, though.'

'Oh, she's delighted, believe me! You've given her a new lease of life. We're all very glad to see that.' There was a short pause as they both sat, relaxing in each other's company. 'And how about the flashbacks? Have they been recurring?'

'Not really. I have been having bad dreams, though. They're really scary, but at least I know they're just dreams. I'm not confused the way I used to be. I know that was only because so much pressure was building up at school. I think things have changed too much now for the flashbacks to come back.'

'That's good to hear. But I'd like you to keep that appointment I've made for you at the Southern. The doctors there will check everything out, just in case.'

'I will.'

'And the future? Are you missing your friends?' As she asked this question, Mrs Conway was watching Mel closely. She knew that body language spoke louder, and often truer, than words. She noted that Mel had shifted her position, and took it as a sign that she was troubled.

There was silence for a moment, then Mel said, 'I don't want to appear ungrateful; being here is great and I never thought I could have it so good.' Suddenly Mel looked up and Mrs Conway saw that her eyes were red and filled with tears. Mel looked earnestly at Mrs Conway. 'It's just that I'm so *lonely*. I miss everybody – not just my dad and my brother, but my friends at school too.'

'Well, why don't you speak to them?

'They wouldn't want anything to do with me. I'm . . .' Mel searched for the right word. 'I'm a *fake*!'

'You misled them, Mel. But you weren't trying to take advantage of them or to cheat them in any way. You were just trying to protect yourself. In the wrong way, granted, but good friends will understand, and will want to rally round. Isn't that what friendship's all about?'

'I suppose so.'

'Would you like to see them again?'

'I'd like to, but . . .'

'Right! That's settled.' With that, Mrs Conway reached into her handbag and took out her mobile. She pressed a button once, listened for the preset number to connect, then disconnected almost immediately. She put her phone back in her bag and sat back with a smile. Mel was baffled.

Suddenly, the front door burst open. Mel couldn't believe her eyes. Julie, Nick, Raj and Angelo tumbled into the room, yelling, 'Surpri-ise!' Julie was holding up a birthday cake with sixteen candles on it. The boys carried an array of gift bags and presents done up in bright wrapping paper.

'Great to see you, Mel,' said Nick, coming over and kissing her on the cheek. Raj and Angelo followed suit. Julie put the cake down on the coffee table and then she and Mel held each other closely.

'Oh, Mel, we've been so worried!' Both girls burst into tears.

'*Mama mia!*' exclaimed Angelo, and, proud of his Latin temperament, he joined in.

Raj and Nick looked at each other. Nick thumped Raj. 'Don't *you* start next!'

'Wouldn't dream of it! Why don't you make yourself useful and organise the prezzies?'

'Good idea.' Nick busied himself, grateful for a diversion, as he suspected it was only a matter of time before he broke down too.

'Come on, Raj, you can give me a hand,' called Mrs Conway from the kitchen. She had discreetly left the room when the others arrived. Moments later, she and Raj came through with trays full of sandwiches and other assorted goodies. 'Irene prepared these before you got up, Mel. She had them hidden away.'

Raj returned to the kitchen and came back out with soft drinks.

'But it's not my birthday!' was all Mel could say.

'Well, we heard about your real one,' said Julie. 'So we thought we'd make up for it.'

'OK, everyone, let Mel open her prezzies first and then we can tuck in. And I think there's someone else to come, isn't there?' said Nick's mum.

'Victoria?' asked Mel.

'Er, I'm afraid she and Nick had a bit of a fall out over her interpretation of events,' said Julie. 'But she assured me she would come . . . separately. She's dying to see you, Mel. But hey, let's get these parcels opened!'

A few minutes later, Mel was surrounded by heaps of wrapping paper, in the midst of which were CDs, earrings, a necklace, toiletries, folders and pens, a blouse . . . and the last gift Mel opened was a beautiful new watch.

'That's from my gran,' said Nick.

'It's gorgeous! I wish she'd stayed,' said Mel, holding it up and showing it off to everyone.

'No, she wanted you to have time on your own,' said Mrs Conway. 'I'm just here to make sure you all clear up!'

The doorbell rang and Mrs Conway went to answer it. Julie's eyes brightened. 'I hope that's . . .'

Mrs Conway showed Victoria in. 'Hi, everybody! Sorry I'm late. Happy belated birthday, Mel!' She walked over and hugged Mel tightly.

'Oh no!' groaned Nick, as the crying started all over again.

'I wish you'd told us at school when it was your birthday,' Victoria said.

'But then you would have expected to see my presents from home and maybe to come out and visit me . . .' Mel's voice trailed off as she realised the implications of what she was saying. She broke down again. 'Can you ever forgive me?'

'We've nothing to forgive,' said Victoria. 'You didn't do us any harm . . . apart from making us worry about you. If only we'd known about your problems!'

'I understand that now. It's just that I was determined to make something of myself . . . I'm *really* sorry!'

'Don't worry,' said Julie. 'We're sorry about all your troubles, of course, but just think: if you come back to school and put all this behind you . . . that would be so cool! You might even be able to look back on it all as . . .' Julie was momentarily lost for words, '. . . as a cool adventure!'

Mel's friends all laughed, but Mel looked downcast. She appreciated her friend's attempt to turn her dreadful experience into something more positive, but she felt things were more complicated than her friends knew. 'There's still the money I've got to pay back. I'll need to work. And I enrolled under a false address, with made-up parents.'

Mrs Conway was trying to keep her distance, but at this point she felt she had to interrupt. 'Mel, actually, Irene's paid it all back already. She was going to tell you herself. She does want you to pay it back to her – only because it would be better for *you* to do that. But you can repay it over a longer period of time. That way you can go back to school and get on your feet. You can get a part-time job if you want, but school is the most important thing.'

'So, you'll be back on Monday? I mean, how are we supposed to get through these prelims without you?' asked Nick.

'Looks like if it was up to you lot I'd have no choice,' said Mel. 'But Mr Hamilton might have something else to say. If he'll let me, I'll come back.'

'Fingers crossed!' said Julie.

Victoria stood up in her usual theatrical fashion. 'And now, I have an announcement to make . . .' she said, 'Ta ra!' With a flourish, she held up her left wrist. 'What do you see? Or to be more precise, what do you *not* see?'

'Your bracelet. You're not wearing your bracelet!' said Mel.

'*Exactement*! Disappeared. Vanished. Crystals no more!'

'What's happened?' asked Nick.

'From now on,' said Victoria grandly, 'the supernatural is going to be an area of interesting speculation – nothing more.'

'You mean . . .'

'Yes, from now on you lot will have to do without my wisdom on these matters. It's your loss!' And with another flourish she sat down amidst everybody's laughter.

'Well done, Victoria,' whispered Julie. 'You handled that brilliantly!'

The conversation drifted on as everyone tucked in. Mel was quite happy to answer questions about her flashbacks.

'Why do you think they started at Athole Gardens?' asked Angelo.

'Yeah, I examined the place but there was nothing unusual that I could see. Why there?' asked Raj.

'I'm not sure, but if you look directly above the gate, you'll see a flat with a beautiful bay window. The room always looked so warm and inviting, everything that my home was not,' replied Mel. 'I used to stop and gaze up at it – just wishing! And I think it started from there.'

Eventually Mrs Conway made a point of taking Mel aside. 'I think it's safe to say you've overcome your fears about your friends, Mel.'

'Oh, they're fantastic! They're all speaking to me just as they did before.' Her face clouded slightly. 'Now the only thing I have to worry about is home.' It's funny, thought Mel. Every time something good like this happens to me, other worries jump out from the back of my mind. There's always got to be something . . .

'One step at a time,' said Mrs Conway. 'It will be a long time before things are totally right. They might never be perfect, but you can learn to cope with that.'

She turned to go back to the others and Mel hung back for a moment before following her.

'OK, everybody! Are we going to eat this cake or not?'

Soon the sixteen candles were flickering merrily and everyone was gathered round in anticipation. 'After three,' called Victoria. 'One, two, three . . .' They all joined in:

> *'Happy Birthday to you!*
> *Happy Birthday to you!*
> *Happy Birthday, dear Me-el,*
> *Happy Birthday to you!'*

'OK, Mel, make a wish and blow!'
Mel made her wish.
And blew out every candle with one big breath.

Chapter 21

During the mid-morning break on Monday, Mel, Victoria and Julie were standing outside the head teacher's office. Mel had just arrived. Victoria squeezed her hand. 'Go for it, Mel.'

Mel knocked on the door as politely as she could. When the green light at the side of the door flashed the word 'Enter', she took a deep breath. She was instantly reminded of when she'd blown out the candles on Saturday. She pushed open the door and walked in.

'Ah, Melissa, come on in,' said Mr Hamilton from behind his desk.

Mel smiled nervously as a woman sitting across from him rose to greet her. 'Nice to see you again, Aunt

Elizabeth,' said Mel, and kissed her lightly on the cheek.

'You too, Melissa. And I mean that. I'd no idea things had got so bad. I should never have lost touch with you the way I did. I'm so sorry!'

'Sit down beside your aunt, Melissa,' said the head teacher, indicating a chair. 'Now, your aunt and I have had a long talk, and Mrs Conway was in earlier. I've made it clear that I was very disappointed about the deception, but I can fully appreciate it was done with the best intentions. Actually, there was no need for the deception. I've checked with our Legal Department, and as long as your aunt had your father's consent – which she obviously did – she was quite entitled to sign the Placing Request.'

'I'm afraid I persuaded her to tell the fib,' said Mel. 'I didn't want anyone to know I came from Morton Street. I just wanted to come here and have a fair chance with the others.'

'Well, your Placing Request is still valid; I'll just change the record to show that your Aunt Elizabeth is your main Contact Person.'

Mel's mouth fell open. 'Does that mean . . . Does that mean I can stay here?'

'Yes, Melissa. I don't think any purpose would be served by excluding you. I'm prepared to accept that you didn't know what you were doing when you walked

154

out with the cash. You took steps to return it and you've agreed to counselling. Mrs Conway and I would like you to take a few days off now to recover, then I hope we can draw a line under the whole sorry business.'

'Thanks, Mr Hamilton. I won't let you down.'

'And if you like, Melissa,' said Aunt Elizabeth, you can start coming down to visit Uncle Jim and me. I know it won't be easy at first, but we can all make an effort to get to know each other. Maybe it's not too late to help Barry either.' Her eyes filled up slightly. 'I'm so sorry for losing touch. I was so angry with Hugh and your mother, but I should have thought more about you and Barry.'

'I can understand how you feel,' said Mel. 'I get angry too. At times when I think of my mum I get white hot with rage. Barry and I loved her so much, but when I think back there are more and more memories that disturb me . . . Times when she never put a decent meal on the table, and sometimes our clothes weren't ready for school, things like that. All because she was slipping into her drugs habit.'

They talked for a good while longer, and then Aunt Elizabeth asked if she could take Mel out for an early lunch. 'Di Maggio's do a great pizza,' said Mel.

Mr Hamilton smiled. 'Then go and enjoy it.'

* * *

The bell for the last lesson before lunch had just rung, but instead of heading for their next class, Victoria and Julie went down to the main foyer where they'd arranged to meet Mel.

'Well, how did it go?' asked Julie, breathless.

'Brilliant! We're going for a pizza,' said Mel. Her aunt moved a little further down the hall to give Mel and her friends some space.

'Not *that*. You know perfectly well!'

'How did what go?'

'Mel, we're going to strangle you!' said Victoria.

'Sorry!' laughed Mel. 'Yes, he's letting me stay.' Her friends let out a cheer and gave Mel a hug. 'Actually, he was really nice about it. I can't believe it! He even said it wouldn't be held against me when I need a reference. Looks like I might make it to uni after all!'

'Ye-es!' The girls gave each other high fives.

'Er . . . there's just one more thing.' Mel looked embarrassed. 'Mr Hamilton's not going to broadcast this round the staff – and I don't really want other kids to know my life story either . . . I've stopped making things up, but can we keep all this quiet?'

'No problem,' Victoria assured her.

'And I know the boys will feel the same way,' added Julie.

'Thanks . . .'

'You girls!' a familiar voice screeched along the corridor. 'What are you doing?'

'We're just on our way to class, Mrs McLaren,' called Victoria. They moved off, giggling as they went, and Mel rejoined her aunt.

Mel got off the Underground at Govan and made her way around to the Social Work Department. Brian Jackson had arranged for the two of them, plus a female colleague, to visit Morton Street and speak with Mel's dad. She wasn't looking forward to it. She was dreading having to face Hughie after all that had happened. Now there was no putting it off.

Mel reported at the desk, and a middle-aged lady with dark, curly hair and glasses came around to greet her. 'Hi, Mel. I'm Terri. I'll be going with you and Brian today.'

Brian came out of his office. 'Mel,' he said, 'how was school?'

'Surprisingly easy. They were all great. It was as if I'd never been away.'

'Fantastic! Now let's see how we get on with your dad.'

'I hope he'll be there,' said Mel, knowing from bitter experience how unreliable Hughie could be.

'Oh, I think he will. I arranged for the Home Help to call this afternoon – to make sure he stayed put, more than anything.' He winked at Mel and all three laughed. 'Right, let's get to the car.'

As they drove into Morton Street, Mel felt a familiar sense of suffocation. A flood of memories came back, causing her to wonder for a moment if the events of the last few days had been real. Surely she was about to come down to earth with a bump and find that she was back to Square One?

Brian parked outside the house and Mel led them to the door. She went in and was more than surprised to see Hughie, shaved and neatly dressed, standing there to greet her. 'How are you, my darlin'? It's good to see you.' He gave her a hug.

'I'm fine, Dad. But how are you? I thought you'd be really angry with me for leaving and getting social workers involved.'

'Ach, I miss you right enough, but I'm glad to think of you making a better life for yourself. You don't deserve to be stuck here with the likes of me and him.' Hughie managed a wry smile.

After Mel had introduced the visitors and they had sat down in the living room, instinctively she offered them tea or coffee. She was relieved when they said not to bother, as she didn't really want to see what state the kitchen might be in.

Brian got the ball rolling. 'Now, Mr Nicol,' he began, 'It was good of you to see us. As you know, Melissa-Jane has asked us to help her with the situation she finds herself in.'

'If you're trying to help our Jane, that's fine by me.'

'She and I have had quite a few chats, Mr Nicol, and one thing is very clear to me and my colleagues: your daughter loves you very much.'

'I can't think why. But I'm very glad to hear it,' said Hughie with a sad look in his eyes.

'Well, you see, it presents us with a bit of a problem,' Mel heard Brian Jackson say. 'It would be easier for everybody if she *didn't* love you. She's sixteen now and she could have the type of voluntary supervision she's agreed to, without the added complication of her family. But since she *does* love you and her brother very much, she worries. It makes her ill thinking about what's happening to both of you.

'It's not an option for her to carry on as before – all that cooking, cleaning, going short of cash, being exposed to drug and alcohol abuse. That was driving her round the bend, wasn't it, Mr Nicol?'

Mel felt her palms becoming clammy.

'Yes, I agree with you. You're going in with the boot, aren't you? But I have to agree with everything you say,' replied Hughie. 'Barry and me – I suppose you could say we're a couple of losers. God only knows where he is just now. Jane doesn't need that hassle.'

'But if she can't live *with* you and she can't live *without* you, what other options are open to her? Let me ask you a brutal question, Mr Nicol. Do you love your daughter? Think hard before you answer.'

The question cut through the room like a knife. Mel squirmed on the settee where she was sitting next to Terri. Shouldn't he have asked me to leave the room before asking that? she thought, then glanced at Terri for some sort of acknowledgement. But Terri simply continued to listen as if it was all nothing out of the ordinary. Some things you take for granted and never think about, Mel thought, but now that the question was out there, dangling precariously between Mel and her father, she was afraid of what she might hear.

'Well, Mr Nicol?'

Hughie's face was a picture of indignation, and Mel could see that he was struggling to control himself. For a moment she thought he was going to lash out.

But Brian Jackson pressed on. 'It's better that Melissa knows now, then we can go away and try to deal with it. Do you *not* love your daughter?'

Suddenly Mel caught a withering look on her dad's face that she had seen before. It was like he was collapsing into surrender. Then she saw him turn his head and look directly at her. 'It's not that I *don't* love her. It's . . . it's more that I *can't*. When Rona died, something died inside me too. It was like having your heart gripped by ice. I've felt nothing but despair for the past five years or so, day in and day out. I can't face my children. They know I supplied their mother with drugs. They know I killed her.' He looked back at Brian. 'We all find our own ways to cope, Mr Jackson. And you know what my way is. I've always felt I was too far down that road to turn back.'

'If we could help you find another way, would you be willing to look for it?'

Hughie said nothing. He only raised one eyebrow slightly. To Brian, that was a sign of at least a flicker of interest.

'What your life is lacking just now, Hughie,' – Brian felt the time had come to be more informal – 'is a simple ingredient. It's called *motivation*. Now, supposing you knew *for certain* that you would regain your daughter's respect if you kicked your dependence on drugs and alcohol and got back to work? You don't need to worry about her love; you've got that already. But if you knew that your daughter would *respect* you, and would never hold the past against you; that all she asked was your love in return – would you give it?'

Hughie looked at Mel again. 'If that was possible, I would never ask anything more from life!'

Brian sat back and deliberately said nothing for a while. Then eventually, 'OK. My colleague here has a few suggestions for you, Hughie. It's entirely up to you whether you take her up on them.'

Terri leaned forward on the settee. 'The first thing, Hughie, would be for you to register at the drugs clinic in the hospital . . .'

The rest of the conversation seemed to pass in a blur for Mel. She caught snippets here and there, but mostly she just felt tired. She didn't have the strength to participate in the discussion . . .

'Think of how proud you would be to see your daughter graduate from university. She's bright and she's committed, you know, so it's a distinct possibility. She may even have a family of her own some day. How proud would *she* be to know that her dad was there for her, having fought back from the brink of despair?'

'I want my daughter's respect, but I honestly can't promise that I'll kick this thing. All I can promise is that I'll try.' Hughie turned to Brian and Terri. 'And what about Barry?'

Mel perked up, feeling a sudden wave of optimism.

'Dad, if he saw you making an effort, there's no telling what influence you could have on him.'

Hughie looked sadly at Mel and said softly, 'OK . . . But I can't promise.'

Impulsively, Mel went over and hugged him. 'You've started already!'

Terri made some arrangements for Hughie to register for treatment, then Brian, Terri and Mel got up to leave. 'Are you sure you don't mind me going, Dad? I could stick around for a bit,' asked Mel.

'I lost your mother, and I nearly lost you too. I don't want that, darlin'. So I *want* you to go. I hope you'll come and see me often, but every day you're not here will make me work that bit harder to get my life back. No, you go. If you've got a chance of another life, grasp it with both hands. You can be the inspiration for Barry and me.'

He smiled when she left, but it was a bleak smile that caused Mel to leave with mixed emotions. 'Do you think he'll make it?' she asked when they were back in the car.

'We'll see, Mel,' said Terri. 'We'll give him all the support we can. But at the end of the day, it's up to him. You heard what he said, though. It's time now for you to let go.'

Epilogue

Mel was walking along the pavement towards home. She was pleased with the latest development. She and Irene had hit it off so well together that Irene offered to convert the upstairs of her home into a real flat for Mel. Irene would continue to benefit from the company and the security, and Mel would have her independence. She could visit her family and Ruby as often as she liked.

She opened the front door and quietly went up to her room. From her cupboard she took out the box that contained the mementoes of her mother. She smiled as she fondled them gently. Near the bottom of the box she discovered the Gloria Gaynor tape. She never felt the urge to play it these days. It was a cherished memento, that was all. Funny how life can change, she thought. She was to have her own flat, her dad and her brother were on their recovery programmes, and she was completely settled back at school. University would be the important 'next step' in her life.

But underlying it all was the possibility that Hughie and Barry would find the challenge too great. She shuddered as she remembered her last visit home. There was a distinct smell of alcohol on Hughie's breath, and from all accounts, Barry was still roaming the streets for days on end. She worried about them constantly. However, she had come to realise that their lives were not her life. The situation with her family struck her as both ironic and sad. 'Everyone keeps saying you need the support of a good family,' she had told Irene, 'but the only way for me to have a good life is to be separated from mine!' But whatever the future might hold, she felt that, thanks to the support and love of her friends, she was strengthened and would cope.

Mel replaced the lid on the cardboard box, pushed it gently back into the cupboard, and turned her mind to other things.

Acknowledgements

My thanks go to Brenda and Yasemin at Piccadilly Press for their continued support and encouragement.

Note From the Author

Dissociative Identity Disorder, the medical name for Mel's condition, is becoming more common in young people, and is usually the result of childhood trauma (i.e., painful emotional and/or physical experiences). When there is no obvious way out of a painful situation, a child will sometimes escape into fantasy. This can get out of hand and lead to other symptoms, such as amnesia, depression, mood swings, suicidal tendencies, sleep disorders, panic attacks and phobias. It doesn't always go that far; like other illnesses, there are both severe and mild cases. If you feel that you or any of your friends are inventing a fantasy life that is getting out of control, you could seek help from your school counsellor or family doctor. The condition can be cured.

If you would like more information about books available from Piccadilly Press and how to order them, please contact us at:

Piccadilly Press Ltd.
5 Castle Road
London
NW1 8PR

Tel: 020 7267 4492
Fax: 020 7267 4493

Feel free to visit our website at
www.piccadillypress.co.uk